P9-EES-786

THE SEARCH FOR
BABY RUBY

THE SEARCH FOR
BABY RUBY

ARTHUR A. LEVINE BOOKS
AN IMPRINT OF SCHOLASTIC INC.

Library of Congress Cataloging-in-Publication Data
Shreve, Susan, author.
The search for Baby Ruby / by Susan Shreve. — First edition.
pages cm
Summary: Twelve-year-old Jess O'Fines is resentful that she is expected to watch her baby niece in a Los Angeles hotel room while the rest of her dysfunctional family go off to a wedding rehearsal party — but when Baby Ruby disappears, Jess is convinced she knows who kidnapped her and determined to get her back on her own, whatever the danger.
ISBN 978-0-545-41783-9 (hardcover : alk. paper) 1. Kidnapping — Juvenile fiction. 2. Infants — Juvenile fiction. 3. Nieces — Juvenile fiction. 4. Dysfunctional families — Juvenile fiction. 5. Los Angeles (Calif.) — Juvenile fiction. [1. Kidnapping — Fiction. 2. Babies — Fiction. 3. Nieces — Fiction. 4. Family problems — Fiction. 5. Los Angeles (Calif.) — Fiction.] I. Title.
PZ7.S55915Se 2015
813.54 — dc23
2014033340

10 9 8 7 6 5 4 3 2 1   15 16 17 18 19

Printed in the U.S.A.   23
First edition, June 2015

Book design by Ellen Duda

To Arthur Levine

With admiration and love

CHAPTER ONE

BABY RUBY?

It was the last weekend in May, and in room 618 of the Brambles Hotel in Los Angeles, Jess O'Fines was trying to zip up her new shimmery violet sundress without catching the soft flesh around her belly in the zipper.

"Too tight, babes?" her sister Teddy said.

"Are you saying I'm fat?" Jess asked, holding her breath.

"I'm just wondering if the dress is too *too* small," Teddy said from the plush rose carpet, where she was lying with her eyes closed, her feet on the bed, waiting for the electric-blue nail polish she'd painted on her toes to dry.

"You *do* think I'm fat, don't you, Teddy," Jess said matter-of-factly.

"I think you're yummy and sweet."

"Whatever that means."

"Warm blueberry muffins, delicious carrot cake. You're the best."

"Oh brother . . ."

And just then their real brother, Danny, flew into the room with Baby Ruby under his arm like a football.

"Jess," he said, out of breath, half-dressed, no shirt, his belt unbuckled.

Jess, in that frantic way he had of announcing an emergency, as if he had just exploded all over the hall of the Brambles Hotel.

Jess didn't even lift her head from the job of zipping — her dress *was* a little too tight in the waist, very tight around the rib cage, but she'd been able to fit into it when she tried it on at Lateda Dresses in downtown Larchmont, next door to the wedding dress store where her sister Whee was shopping.

"I have a problem, Jessie," Danny said.

"Me too," Jess said. "I'm trying to get dressed for the party tonight."

All year, Jess had been waiting for this weekend in Los Angeles, for staying at a hotel with room service, something she had never done before. There would be parties before the wedding and after the wedding and dancing and a swimming pool and the Pacific Ocean hammering the beach just outside the hotel balcony.

A normal family occasion like the ones she'd read about in books ever since she could remember, or seen on television and in other families in the neighborhood, or mostly dreamed about before she went to sleep at night.

"Bad news, babes!" Danny's plump panda-bear face was white with shaving cream. "I've got to have your help."

"It's my twelfth birthday," Jess replied without looking up. "I *can't* help you."

"*Yesterday* was your twelfth birthday, Jess, and I told you I have an amazing present in my suitcase for you that you'll love."

He took a sniff of Baby Ruby's diaper and made a face.

"*This* is an emergency," he said.

Jess had zipped the dress all the way up but she could barely breathe.

"A *heart-stopping* emergency."

Danny O'Fines often had *heart-stopping* emergencies. Squash for the baby's lunch burning on the stove, a fire in the washing machine, his keys dropped in the trash can and lost, Baby Ruby twice slipping off the bed while Danny was shaving or searching in the closet for the *right* shirt for the day. He was a stay-at-home dad with nothing to do but take care of Baby Ruby and go on the Internet to look for jobs while his bad-tempered wife, Beatrice, called Beet, was in medical school.

"This is the deal," Danny began, taking a diaper out of the back pocket of his dress trousers. "I had everything organized with the hotel — the babysitter was coming at six thirty to our hotel room, 642. I called from home weeks ago and they said, 'DONE, Mr. O'Fines. A babysitter will be knocking on your door at six thirty,' they said. Her name is something like Melinda or Belinda or Melissa. And there I am waiting for this truant, and nobody, not even housekeeping, appears. So I check the front desk of the hotel and they tell me 'BAD NEWS, Mr. O'Fines.' So, the babysitter we got for Baby Ruby blew us off."

"Get another one," Jess said.

"There isn't another one. I asked at the front desk."

"In the whole city of Los Angeles?"

Jess sat down on the end of the king-sized bed she was sharing with her sisters for the weekend.

This was the kind of thing that happened to Jess O'Fines, the youngest of the O'Fines kids, the baby in the family by three years, the only child left at home with their mother, Delilah, after the divorce was final and Teddy was sent to live at the home for juvenile delinquent girls to recover from kleptomania.

Tonight Jess was supposed to be wearing her violet dress and strappy high-heeled sandals to the rehearsal dinner in the hotel's Bay Room overlooking the Pacific Ocean. Every single other person in her family would be there. Her brother and sisters and aunts and uncles, her cousins, her mother and father, and her mother's best friend and her father's tennis partner. She was *supposed* to be sitting at the head table between Whee, who would be marrying Victor Treat the next day in the garden of the Brambles Hotel, and her father, Aldie O'Fines, formerly Daddy.

Jess was Aldie's *date* for the weekend.

Danny plopped Baby Ruby down on the bed beside Jess.

"You can bring the baby to the rehearsal dinner," Jess said.

"I can't!" he said, changing Baby Ruby's poopy diaper right there on the white sheets. "I have to make a speech."

"What about Beet?" Jess asked.

"Beet?" He rolled his eyes. "You know Beet better than that. She's not an option to babysit in the hotel room."

"Beet is the *man* in the family," her father had said when the computer company for which Danny worked downsized, and Danny lost his job and became the "at home" parent. "Danny is the mother," her father had said.

"I'm not an option for babysitting either," Jess said, running her hand through her slightly curly hair, tears of frustration welling in her eyes.

Already she could feel her plans for the evening unraveling around her and there was nothing she could do about it. She was the fail-safe child, the last child at home with hand-me-down clothes and leftover dinners when her mother went on a date, and tonight Jess was stuck with someone's leftover job.

"JESS!"

Delilah opened the door to room 618 and slipped in, dragging a Pack and Play for Baby Ruby and dressed in a tiny fuchsia strapless thing so tight she could barely walk.

"The *major* speech, Jess. Danny is giving the major speech of the evening to his sister Louisa," her mother said, catching sight of herself in the mirror over the dresser.

"Is this dress too tight?"

Delilah turned around, checking the mirror over her shoulder so she could see her behind.

"It *is* too tight, isn't it, everyone?"

"Yes," Teddy said. "But that shouldn't stop you."

"I would rather not babysit," Jess said quietly, sitting on the edge of the bed.

"*Of course* you would rather not babysit, darling. . . ." Her mother hesitated, leaning into the mirror to examine her mascara. "But honestly, Jess, you know the dinner will be dull with speeches and blah, blah, blah, and you'll be doing Danny and all of us who adore you such a favor."

"I plan to be at the rehearsal dinner," Jess said, but even as she spoke, she knew she had lost.

If only Jess were able to cry on demand in a pinch like her friends could do. Just once, she wished she could be the kind of girl who lost her temper or caused a scene or fell to the floor in tears. Or be like Teddy, who would say to her only mother, *You've got to be kidding. I am not going to miss the rehearsal dinner just because Danny asked me to babysit his child as if I were some kind of servant. He's your son, so maybe you should be the one to babysit."*

Teddy could do that. But Jess simply wasn't that kind of girl.

She didn't complain. She didn't say *I can't* with a mouthful of tears the way other girls might do. And she didn't ever say NO!

"What's the matter with *no*," Teddy had asked her once. "It's a good word."

"I can't say no, especially to Mom," Jess said. "Just in case."

"Just in case what?" Teddy had asked.

"Just in case Mom puts me up for adoption."

"Unlikely."

✦

As far as her family was concerned, Jess was perfectly happy. Or else she had persuaded herself that she was happy. But she had bad thoughts. She couldn't help it. Right now she was thinking she could bolt out the door of room 618. *Bye, bye, Ruby O'Fines,* she'd wave at Baby Ruby lying in her Pack and Play — after all, what could happen to a baby in a Pack and Play? Off Jess would go, down in the elevator, past the room where the rehearsal dinner was taking place just as Danny was giving his stupid speech, out the back door of the hotel, across the beach, and surely in this beautiful hotel, she would meet a boy, maybe a little older, and he'd ask her to swim in the moonlight and she'd take off her dress and jump in the inlet just off the Pacific Ocean, swimming next to him without a single thought of Baby Ruby.

Across the room, Teddy sat on the floor in her underwear, watching the television on mute.

"You're toast, Jess," she said.

Toast was Teddy's new word for everything. Even Whee was *toast* for getting married.

"You'll be spending the evening right here in room 618 while the rest of us are yukking it up at Whee's rehearsal dinner."

"*You* could watch the baby, Teddy," Jess said. "You don't even *like* parties."

"They wouldn't let me," Teddy said, lighting a thin, ebony European cigarette. "I'm a juvenile delinquent."

"No smoke allowed around the baby," Danny called. "And while you're at it, Teddy, don't sit around in your underwear with a man in the room."

"A man in the room?" Teddy asked. "I hadn't noticed. Is there a man in this room, Jess? All I can see is Danny. And Mom, of course, doing her lipstick."

Jess shrugged.

That's the way her family had been since she was in second grade.

Divorced parents, unemployed brother with a grumpy wife and a baby, a juvenile-delinquent high-school-dropout sister sprung just for the weekend from reform school, where she was spending a few months for shoplifting again and again and again.

"Okay, babes?" Danny said, ruffling Jess's hair, dropping Baby Ruby in her lap. He opened a diaper bag and took out bottles and rattles and wipes. "My favorite, *good-as-gold* little sister."

"Your *demented* little sister," Jess said, wriggling around so Ruby could fit into the cup of her lap. "Weak, wimpy little sister. I should run away."

"Here are two bottles of milk," Danny said. "Beet's breast milk. She froze it."

"Oh, swell!" Jess said. "Good to know."

"Give Ruby one bottle at eight, one at midnight." Danny ignored her comment.

"Midnight?"

Danny checked his hair in the mirror.

"How come you're getting back so late?" Jess asked, a sinking feeling in her stomach.

"It's a late party, Jess," Teddy said, turning off the television. "I plan to have a panic attack at about ten o'clock and call 911."

"Here are diapers," Danny was saying, scrounging the bottom of the diaper bag. "Feed her, burp her, change her into jammies, put her

9

in the Pack and Play, and pray she doesn't scream bloody murder. But Jess." Danny lifted her chin. "Look at me. Do not EVER take your eyes off the baby under any circumstances."

She took a deep breath.

"The Brambles is a hotel," Danny said, as if Jess were brain-dead, as if it had not already come to her attention that she was in a hotel. "And anything can happen to a baby in a hotel."

"Thanks, Danny," she said. "I kind of guessed we must be in a hotel."

Danny gave a thumbs-up and, without another word, he and Delilah left.

"Think of it this way, Jess," Teddy was saying. "At least you won't be there when Mom's dress splits right up the back and she has to wrap herself in the tablecloth."

The door to the bathroom opened and Whee walked out, a towel wrapped around her chest, crying as she seemed to be doing ever since she and Victor had decided to get married.

"What's happening *now*?" Whee asked.

"Just the usual O'Fines family fun and games," Teddy said.

"Like what fun and games?"

"We've been playing Scrabble, singing old school songs, hugging and kissing and dancing," Teddy said. "As for me, I'm having a blast, Whee, just like you seem to be doing."

"Whee's *not* having a blast," Jess said. "She cries every day."

"From happiness," Teddy said. "Happiness just gets to some people and they cry all the time."

"You guys . . . leave me alone," Whee said, collapsing on the bed. "STOP!"

Jess worried about things. She worried that Whee wasn't crying from *happiness*, that Danny and Beet would have a terrible fight as usual and Beet would leave with Baby Ruby and go back to Larchmont, that Teddy would live in reform school for the rest of her life, that after Delilah finally got the boyfriend she was looking for in her tight dresses, she, Jessica O'Fines, would end up like the bag ladies on the Avenue in Larchmont with all of her possessions loaded in a grocery cart, sleeping the nights in a trash bag next to the CVS.

She worried that maybe *marriage* in the O'Fines family would never work out for any of them.

"I hate this family," Whee said, flinging her arm over her eyes.

"Ditto," Teddy said. "But this family is the one you have, unless you plan to take on Victor Treat's family of robots as your very own."

"That's exactly what I plan to do," said Whee. "And I plan to live in a clean house with dinner on time and the laundry done, and I plan to have ordinary, well-behaved children and love my husband until death do us part. Which will certainly be a change from *this* family."

"Whew!" Teddy said, getting up to dress. "That's too many plans."

"And what is Baby Ruby doing here?" Whee asked, exasperated.

"The babysitter bailed," Jess said.

"Of course she bailed," Whee said. "Danny probably made the arrangements for the wrong date."

Jess picked up Baby Ruby and sat on a chair across from the bed.

"I'm glad you're going to be married until death do you part," Jess said. "I was beginning to wonder."

"I'm emotional." Whee sat on the bed, rubbing her eyes. "It's emotional to get married. You'll know about that when you do it."

"I'm emotional without getting married," Jess said, pressing her nose against Baby Ruby's warm cheek.

"And I'll never get married," Teddy said. "It's enough trouble to live with myself."

There was a knock on the door and Aldie O'Fines, in a blazer and striped shirt with a red-and-blue Superman tie, stuck his head in the room.

"Hurry up, guys. The party's on."

"I'm going to be late, Dad," Whee said. "And tell Danny *thanks a lot* for making Jess take care of Baby Ruby."

"Anything I can do to help you girls?" Aldie asked, ignoring Whee. "A glass of wine. A new car? You guys get dressed pronto, and Jess O'Fines, my date for the weekend? *You're a champ!*"

He shut the door and headed to the elevators. They could hear him whistling all the way down the hall.

~

Whee stood in front of the mirror in her lacy black dress, holding her long blond hair up.

"What do you think? Should I wear it up or down?"

"It looks beautiful down, Whee," Jess said.

"I could cut it off in a rat pixie like mine," Teddy said, joining her sister at the mirror. "I've got scissors in my suitcase."

She was taller than Whee and skinny, too skinny, her face white as chalk. But she had pale blond hair like Whee's and "good bones," as their mother had told them both, and might even be pretty if she made an effort.

"Soon you'll lose your baby fat like Teddy," Delilah had said to Jess, "and then your good bones will show up."

"Baby fat?"

Sometimes, her mother drove her crazy.

What Jess saw when she looked in the full-length mirror was not *baby fat*. It was FAT — a squishy ball of flesh in the middle of her torso ruffling the waist of her violet dress; a round, freckled face; slightly curly hair tumbling down to her shoulders; and bright blue eyes. She liked her eyes.

Whee reached out her hand to Jess.

"Come look at the perfect O'Fines sisters before I leave the tribe and become Louisa Treat."

"You won't be Whee any longer?" Jess asked, standing next to her, holding Baby Ruby in her arms so all that showed of Jess was her face and arms and legs but not the little rolls of fat around her belly.

"I'll always be Whee to you guys." She shook her long hair, kissed Jess on the head, and grabbed Teddy by the hand, heading for the door.

"Good-bye, Jess. I am so sorry about our completely incompetent brother." She checked the clock on the counter. "We're late!"

"Late is good," Teddy was saying as they hurried down the hall to the elevators.

Jess stood in the doorway, watching her sisters.

The corridor was empty except for a small man — young, a little plump, but cute. Cute, like a little boy, with black hair and straight-across bangs. He was wearing jeans and a bright green shirt with a button-down collar and the sleeves folded up. He looked as if he was waiting for the elevator, but when the elevator stopped at the sixth floor, when Teddy and Whee got in and disappeared, the small man was still standing beside the elevators. Then, with the snap of the closing doors, he turned toward Jess as if he was headed in her direction.

Instinctively, she backed into the room, shut the door, and put Baby Ruby on her back in the middle of the bed.

Then, returning to the door, she opened it a crack, just enough to see the same man, now in sunglasses, peering down the hallway, and then, as if on cue, Baby Ruby started to scream her high-pitched, breathless cry. Jess rushed back to the bed to pick Ruby up, walking her back and forth across the room to stop her tears.

～

When Ruby settled down, Jess put her on a towel on the carpeted floor, watching her raise her tiny arms in the air to examine her hands.

Four months old, round and pink, with cotton-puff yellow hair that stuck straight up, little red lips like a circle drawn where the mouth belonged, and soon, soon, maybe before the eight p.m. bottle — Jess knew from experience — Baby Ruby would be crying bloody murder, because that is what she did.

Danny had left Beet's breast milk on the counter of the kitchenette. In the light pouring through the window, the milk was bluish white and thin, not at all like milk, and Jess wondered if all breast milk was like this or possibly only Beet's milk — pale sourpuss Beet O'Fines, making washed-out blue milk.

She put the bottles in the tiny fridge, took a package of M&M's

from the hospitality basket on the counter, and ate them one by one, watching Ruby O'Fines do nothing at all but stare at the overhead light and make little sounds of *ooooooooo* and *aaaaaaaaa* and *mmmmmm* in the back of her throat.

Jess checked the clock beside the bed. Seven o'clock, an hour before the bottle, before Danny O'Fines would be giving his important toast to Whee, who would be crying. In Jess's chair at the head table, next to Aldie, Teddy would be preparing to have a panic attack.

She stopped, shhhed Baby Ruby, and there Teddy was — *whoop* — beeping on Jess's cell phone.

You okay? Teddy had written. **Having fun?**

Jess rolled over on her stomach and hit the REPLY button on her phone.

> **Baby Ruby is blah blah blahing away on the floor. Beet's breast milk is sitting on the counter and I'm thinking of leaving this hotel room for Paris. And you?**

There was a beep before Jess even sat up.

Having a blast, Teddy had written. **PANIC ATTACK! The EMTs should be here any minute.**

Jess flipped her cell phone shut and hung over the bed watching Baby Ruby, whose little round legs were waving in the air as she reached out hopelessly to catch a foot.

"Hi, Ruby," Jess said.

"Mmmmmmm," Ruby replied.

"Hungry?"

"Mmmmmmm."

"The only thing I have here is Beet's breast milk and I can't imagine that's good for you."

"Oooooo."

"Just you and me, Ruby, not invited to the party."

"Oooooo."

"Exactly. Maybe it's good for you so far, but that'll change pretty soon. Look at me, in a hotel room taking care of a baby when my new dress is stuffed in a suitcase all by itself."

Jess slid off the bed and lay down next to Ruby, chin in hand, watching the baby girl smiling her furtive little smile, her lips turned up like quotation marks, a dimple in one corner of her mouth.

"I'm very sorry about your father, my brother, my imbecile brother. If you'd looked for all the possible fathers to choose from, you could have done a great deal better."

"Mmmmm."

Baby Ruby was getting sleepy — a long stare, her eyelids fluttering, her hand playing with her ear.

"We'll find the perfect father for you, lamb chop," Jess whispered in a singsong voice. "And then we can ditch your mother and I'll take her place. We'll travel. We'll get a dog."

Another *whoop* and Jess opened her cell phone to Teddy's new message.

> **Listen Jess. I have a thought — do something BIG like bolt the hotel. Take Baby Ruby with you. Maybe even Whee's wedding dress. You might find it useful in Paris.**

Jess lay down on the carpet, watching Baby Ruby, whose eyes were closed but fluttering. It was seven thirty, a little after, and she was thinking maybe Teddy was right — she should do something, not exactly something big, but she did have time to do something like try out Whee's new makeup.

At least Whee shouldn't mind if she *tried on* the makeup. Just a little.

Not the wedding dress.

She opened the door quickly, closed it, and turned on the light.

The bathroom was huge, with a mirror that stretched across the double sink, a shower with a glass door, a bathtub, and a bidet, which Jess had never seen before, but this was her first trip to California. The bidet looked to Jess like a small toilet for children, perhaps. The sink counter held Whee's makeup bag, a small suitcase, and her wedding shoes, which were red satin, pencil-thin high heels.

She opened the suitcase, blue with a blue silky lining, and inside she found white lace bikini underwear, a strapless bra, a blue garter, an old lace handkerchief, and, in a jewel box, a diamond on a slender chain.

Jess looked at herself in the wide mirror behind the sink. Her body was larger than she remembered when they had left Larchmont for the airport just that morning. Even her face, normally a regular face, not even plump, with a shadow of cheekbones and no double chin, looked as if it had spread in the last twelve hours. She unzipped her sundress and stepped out of it. Took off her underwear and stood on the toilet so she could examine herself in full in the mirror.

What she saw was not good news. All she had had to eat since she'd left home was a bag of chips on the plane and two orange juices, chicken salad for lunch with one muffin and butter and jam, and a chocolate milk shake with Teddy after they arrived at the hotel. There was no reason for her to expand this quickly in a single day.

She hopped off the toilet, opened the door very slowly to check on Baby Ruby, who was sleeping just as she had been when Jess went in the bathroom. She hung her sundress on a hook and closed the door again.

Whee's wedding dress was hanging in a large plastic bag in the shower *to steam out the wrinkles*, Whee had told her.

"The dress is a secret," Whee had told Jess.

"From everyone?" Jess asked.

"Pretty much. Only Mom has seen it."

Jess unzipped the bag.

The dress was strapless, with tiny pearls scattered like raindrops across the bodice. She pulled it out of the bag — carefully, carefully — Whee would kill her — and held it up to her own body, which was not so tall.

Then she picked up the makeup bag, set it on the sink, and turned on the water.

Every kind of makeup was there, as if Whee had stripped the cosmetic store of its stock — lipsticks, lip gloss, mascara in two colors, eyeliner, lip liner in four colors, eye shadow in sky blue and turquoise, concealer, foundation, loose powder, blush. Jess set it all out on the sink counter and started with foundation. She poured it in her palms, rubbed her hands together, and spread it across her face. In the mirror, under the bright light, it concealed the multitude of freckles across her nose and cheeks. Then she traced her eyelids with the dark blue eyeliner, the way she'd seen Whee and her mother do, brushed on sky-blue eye shadow, and applied mascara, which she had to put on twice because it smudged. The water was still running but Jess wasn't aware of the sound any longer, wasn't even aware of Baby Ruby sleeping in the next room, or whether she might be crying, or even if she could hear her if she did.

Slowly, she transformed her small, freckled face into a thing of beauty. A face for the fashion magazines that Whee leafed through, looking at the pictures of models with their pouty mouths and wide eyes.

She chose raspberry lipstick, peach blush. In the mirror, she looked beautiful. She put the tops on the makeup and zipped up the bag.

Leaning against the wall, she considered Whee's wedding dress.

It was the most beautiful dress she had ever seen. Did she dare? If she tried it on, really quickly just to see herself in the full-length mirror on the back of the door, would she be sorry? It could be too small, especially around the waist since Whee was thin. It could rip. And then what? And what about Whee? It wasn't Whee's fault that Jess was babysitting during the rehearsal dinner.

She took the white lace strapless bra out of the basket on the bidet and took the wedding dress off its hanger, unzipping the side, the dress over her head, sliding down her arms, her torso. It was heavy, a little stiff, and it almost fit, but she couldn't zip it up because the zipper was in the back. She checked the mirror, adjusted the front of the dress so it lay flat against her chest, her head up, no jewelry, only makeup.

Makeup!

And she'd put the dress on over her head.

Oh god, she thought. Could lipstick or concealer or powder or blush have gotten on the dress? She glanced through half-closed eyes. Nothing, nothing, and then she just saw a tiny mark at the top of the dress, *tiny, tiny, tiny*, she thought, and concealed by the pearls strewn over the front.

Would Whee notice? Or would she be too nervous to notice any-thing except how beautiful she was.

A jumble of thoughts rushed through Jess's mind, and suddenly she remembered that she had left Baby Ruby lying on her back on a terry cloth towel in the middle of the bedroom.

She turned off the water and listened.

Nothing.

Slowly, her heart pounding in her head, warm blood sinking to her feet, a weak sick feeling in her stomach, she opened the bath-room door.

CHAPTER TWO

THE SAVE-THE-MARRIAGE BABY

Jess was seven when her parents announced they were getting a divorce.

It was a Tuesday in June, the week after the Larchmont public schools shut down for the summer, and the family had just grilled hamburgers in the backyard. Dessert was ice-cream sandwiches, Jess's favorite, which she would later throw up on the blue-and-white-striped rug in her bedroom.

All of the O'Fineses were there: Jess, Teddy, Whee, and Danny, in a bad humor since he had made plans to go into the city to meet friends.

"Let's retire to the living room," Aldie had said. "It looks like rain."

"Why do we need to retire at all?" Danny asked. "I've made other arrangements for tonight."

"I told you that your father and I wanted to speak to all of you together after dinner. Did you forget?" Delilah asked.

"I just hoped *you'd* forget," Danny said, following his father into the television room, where they sat, Delilah and Aldie side by side on a piano bench, the children, not exactly still children, sinking into the sectional.

Aldie spoke first, a hitch in his voice as if he were about to weep, something Danny pointed out later.

"Did you check Dad out? He was almost crying. Obviously, this decision was Mom's," he told his siblings.

"After years of deliberation, your mother and I have concluded that we are going to separate," Aldie began, as if he were a stranger reading a script for a play.

"Years of *deliberation*?" Danny asked. "What does that mean?"

"It means that we are taking this *very* seriously and have discussed it for a long time," Delilah said.

"Our family means everything to your mother and me," Aldie added.

Delilah would stay in the family house with Jess and Teddy, who was eleven; Aldie would move to an apartment in New York City; Whee would be leaving for college in a year; and Danny was already a sophomore at Tufts in Boston. Chaucer, the family's black lab, would continue to live with Delilah in Larchmont, although Madeline, the parakeet, would be given away.

Poor Madeline, Jess was thinking. *Why should she suffer when she's just a bird?*

"I want to go back to what you referred to as *years of deliberation*," Danny said. "How *many* years have you been thinking about a divorce?"

Delilah shrugged.

"What do you think, Aldie? Six, seven?"

"Eight," Aldie said with confidence, as if he had in mind a fixed date when the troubles began.

"That's a long time," Whee said.

"I guess there's nothing to say," Danny said.

"You should feel free to ask us anything at all," Aldie said.

Jess made a funny sound in her throat, as if she might be sick.

"I have nothing to ask," Danny said.

"Whee?"

Whee shook her head.

"I'd really like to cut this short," Danny said.

"If that's the way you want it." Aldie glanced at Delilah, who was tapping her fingernails against the wooden bench.

"Girls?" Aldie asked.

But no one spoke.

Jess and Teddy sat on the sectional, pressed together, looking down at their laps.

"Do you girls have any worries?" Aldie asked gently.

"No worries for sure," Teddy said in a tinny voice. "So . . ." She didn't finish.

"So?" Aldie asked.

"So if we're finished with the conversation, why don't you guys go," Teddy said. "Leave the family room."

Aldie got up and clapped his hands together, saying he and Delilah wanted to see the new Woody Allen movie and the family was invited to join them.

"I don't think so," Danny said, finishing the rest of his father's beer. "But have a good time."

The children stood at the south window of the family room and watched their parents climb into the old Volvo and back out of the driveway.

"The movies! What are they thinking about?" Whee asked. "As if tonight, when they've put an end to our lives forever, is just a normal night and off they go in the car to the movies as if nothing whatever has happened."

"So they have been lying to us for eight years?" Teddy asked.

"Not lying exactly," Whee said. "They've been trying to work things out, whatever that means."

"I hate them," Teddy said.

"So, eight years ago. What was going on then?" Danny asked. "I was twelve and had just been asked to repeat sixth grade."

"I was nine," Whee said. "I don't remember. I don't remember anything of my childhood except trying to be perfect all the time. Teddy was almost four."

"And I wasn't born," Jess said.

"That's right," Whee said. "You weren't born until the next May."

Jess collapsed on the sofa and rested her head on Teddy's shoulder.

"So why did they decide to have me if they were thinking of getting a divorce?"

"That's a good question. Why did they?" Danny asked.

"I think I know why," Whee said, sitting in the wing chair next to the sofa. "I mean their marriage was getting unhappy, so what do they do to make it happy? They make another baby to liven things up."

"What does that mean?" Jess asked.

"It means you were a Save-the-Marriage Baby, Jess." Whee kicked off her flip-flops, crossed her legs, and rested her feet on the coffee table.

"A what?" Jess asked.

"A new beautiful little baby is what they were thinking, and then they wouldn't need to get a divorce."

"Brilliant, Whee," Danny said. "I'm sure you're right. Jessica O'Fines, the *Save-the-Marriage Baby*."

And ever after that night when Jess was seven, her siblings called her the Save-the-Marriage Baby, long before Jess even thought about the consequences of divorce or sex or what it was to be a normal girl in a normal family.

"So they didn't really want *me*?" Jess asked.

"They *wanted* you, and they also wanted you to save their marriage," Teddy said.

"Actually, a *failed* Save-the-Marriage Baby is what you are," Danny said, laughing and hugging his little sister as if they all thought it was very funny.

But it wasn't a bit funny to Jess.

So the Save-the-Marriage Baby hadn't worked. The marriage wasn't saved. Her father moved to an apartment in New York City. Her mother stayed in the house with Jess and Teddy and Chaucer, often crying at the dinner table.

And finally, in some complicated way that Jess didn't exactly understand, the divorce became *her* fault.

She had not been good enough or smart enough or pretty enough or strong enough to save her parents' marriage, and so their lives as a family were ruined.

And that was a fact.

CHAPTER THREE

PANIC ATTACK

Teddy was sitting next to her father at the head table in the Bay Room of the Brambles Hotel, watching him wind his short, freckled fingers around the wineglass. Out of the corner of her eye, she glanced at his hair, which had been thin and gray and now was thin and blond.

"Dyed," her mother whispered.

"What kind of man dyes his hair?" Teddy asked.

Delilah shrugged.

"Your father. That kind."

Her father, Aldie O'Fines, was about to get up to give the opening toast for Whee and Victor's rehearsal dinner, beads of perspiration creeping across his bright red face.

Teddy slouched down in her chair.

Whatever it was he had to say would certainly embarrass her. Sentimental or sickly sweet is what she expected and that is exactly what happened when he started to talk about Whee, *my first daughter, my darling baby girl*, his eyes filling with tears.

"I hope he doesn't cry," Delilah was saying.

"Too late," Teddy said. "He's crying."

"Were you listening?" Delilah whispered as Aldie ended his speech, the sweet gardenia smell of her perfume floating under Teddy's nose, making her queasy.

"Louisa Adele O'Fines, light of my life, heart of my heart, good-bye and good luck!" her father said.

"I was listening," Teddy said.

"Pathetic," Delilah said.

Teddy had mixed feelings about her parents, more bad feelings than good ones she had realized when she was dispatched to the Harrisonwood Reform School to be reassembled as an ordinary, normal fifteen-year-old girl. Or the Home for Girls with Problems, as Teddy and Jess called it.

Of the two, she preferred her father.

"No reason," she told her counselor at the Home. "Except he can't help being who he is and my mother can."

The counselor had given her a journal, black with a hard cover and lined paper.

"You are to keep a record of your feelings during the time you're with us," the counselor had said.

"My feelings?" Teddy asked, alarmed.

"Any feelings just as they come to you," the counselor said.

"I'm not going to be doing that," Teddy had said. "I'm not interested in a book about my feelings."

Instead, she used the black journal for lists of food she missed from home, like artichoke hearts and dark chocolate with salty almonds and Starbucks chai lattes. Or places she would go when she was released. New York, maybe California, the beach. And boyfriends. She had had so many of them ever since kindergarten, when Dylan Fry kissed her on the lips.

But the first list in her journal, the one she wrote during the week of her arrival at the Home, ranked the members of her family in order of her affection.

Jess was number one — Teddy's favorite from the start, when her mother brought Jess home wrapped in a pink blanket with a pointy pink hat and dotted red cheeks. *Your new baby*, Delilah had said, and while Teddy was young, she liked to pretend that was true.

My child, my daughter, my little girl, she'd think to herself.

~

Delilah was opening her purse, scrounging for a safety pin.

"I'm afraid the skirt of my dress may have a little tear."

"No kidding!"

"It's not that tight, Teddy. It's supposed to be stretchy. But could you go to the ladies' and check if this hotel supplies safety pins?"

"I may need to go back upstairs," Teddy said.

"Upstairs?"

"To the room."

"And why is that?"

"Because I'm probably going to throw up on the white table-cloth, Mom."

"Please don't, Teddy," Delilah said. "This is your sister's wedding."

"Thanks, Mom. I've picked up on the wedding program."

"Then for once, be normal."

"I'm not normal," Teddy said. "I'm a kleptomaniac."

"But today we should be so happy," Delilah said. "So happy because of Whee and Victor and all of us together on this lovely night."

"We should be happy but we aren't." Teddy pushed her chair away from the table. "As soon as Whee's speech is over, I'll find you a safety pin."

Teddy began shoplifting in the eighth grade. At the time, she didn't call it *shoplifting*. She called it *taking*, and the things she took — clothes, mainly, and cosmetics and jewelry and especially scarves — were things she needed. Not that she needed to *have* them. She needed to *take* them.

She developed a system. She would walk into a shop in Larchmont, wander from front to back, looking at pants and tees, checking the earrings hanging on the metal trees on the front counter. She began with scarves, often at the front of the store in bins, and she'd shuffle through the bins, pick one scarf in particular, glance at the checkout clerk, look around to see if anyone had spotted her, and then stash the scarf in her backpack. Scarves were the easiest, scarves and jewelry, because they didn't have sensors. But as she got better at *taking* during the summer after eighth grade, she took clothes, trying them on behind the dressing room curtain, politely asking a clerk did they have a ladies' room and, once the door was locked, taking out the scissors she kept in her backpack and cutting off the sensor attached to the clothing so an alarm wouldn't sound when she walked out of the store. She'd drop the censor in the container for feminine hygiene installed in the ladies' and walk cheerfully and not too quickly out of the store, calling *Good-bye* and *Thank you*, and head home with a tremendous sense of relief.

At home, she'd stuff her stash in the back of her closet at the bottom of a small trunk that held her childhood toys and stuffed animals and treasures she collected.

"I can't help myself," Teddy told her parents when the manager of the Banana Republic called Delilah to report the shoplifting — *just a warning,* she said, *we won't call the police this time.*

"I go into a store and I *have* to take something," she said.

"If you *have* to take something, don't go into stores," her father said.

"I could promise you I won't, but I know I will," she said. "I can even *promise* I won't take anything, but I will and I do and I don't think I'll ever stop."

On Saturdays, after soccer, Teddy would walk downtown alone, leaving her friends at the coffee shop on Main Street, thinking about what she'd take that day — maybe a dress or a T-shirt or a necklace, nothing too expensive.

Things got worse. She began to wake up in the morning wondering where she would go after school that day. Maybe Tweens and Teens on Main Street. Maybe Lateda. Would she slip it into her backpack in full view of the salespeople, or would she go to the ladies' room or a dressing room? Would she get caught?

She had only been caught twice. The second time was at the drugstore, taking a packet of pens. But the police had never been called and the merchandise had been returned and she'd apologized to the manager.

By the time Teddy was in high school, she was skipping her afternoon classes, heading downtown. She especially liked Lateda, where the clothes didn't have sensors but there was still an element of danger because the shop was small and it was easy for the salesperson to see her drop a skirt or tunic or scarf in her backpack.

Shoplifting required skill, and she was very good at it.

The stores in Larchmont began to expect Teddy O'Fines. She'd saunter in the front door, and since the town was small and people knew one another, she'd wave to the salesladies, call the ones she knew by name. By her sophomore year of high school, she had lost interest in Larchmont. Mid-October, after Columbus Day weekend, she left school at noon, just after Spanish and before lunch. She got on the train from Larchmont to New York City, walked to Saks Fifth Avenue on Fifth Avenue between Fiftieth and Forty-Ninth Street, and took a diamond bracelet from the top of a jewelry counter while the saleslady's back was turned.

She was caught before she could get to the end of the counter.

"I don't dye my hair, if that's why you're looking at me, Teddy," Delilah said.

"I wasn't looking at your hair," Teddy said. "I was looking at your necklace with the big red stone. I've never seen it before."

"Do you like it?

"Actually, no. It's pretty ugly."

"It was Grandma's and it's fake," Delilah said. "Costume jewelry, so never mind stealing it."

"I wasn't thinking of stealing it, Mom," Teddy said, tears welling in her eyes. "How could I steal it if it's around your neck?"

"That shouldn't stop you."

Teddy turned her head away, squeezing her damp eyes shut, wiping her cheeks with the back of her hand.

"I'm having a terrible time at this dinner."

She was trembling.

"Shhh, Ted. Whee's about to speak."

Whee was thanking Aldie for his beautiful toast. She thanked her mother for her energy and optimism, and Danny for his loyalty.

"And thanks to my little sister Jess, who can't be here," Whee said. "And to my next little sister, Teddy."

Thank you, Teddy, for being my little sister.

My troubled little sister, Teddy thought.

"I don't want to shoplift," she had told her parents so many times she couldn't count them.

"Just quit," her father said, while her mother shook her head sadly, as if there had been a death in the family. "Pretty easy solution."

"I try to stop and it doesn't happen. I just do it again."

"Then maybe you should try harder," her father said.

"Like *The Little Engine That Could*. 'I think I can, I think I can, I think I can. . . .' " Delilah had said.

Sometimes, Teddy simply hated her mother. She couldn't help it.

———✂———

The waiters were serving the first course. Cold green soup with a curl of lemon on the top.

Something about the greenness of it, the fact that it was cold, made Teddy gag. She pushed it away.

"I might throw up right now," Teddy said, and she did feel clammy, her body cold and damp. "Truly."

"Well, don't," Delilah said.

At the Home for Girls, no one paid particular attention to Teddy. Everyone there had problems, big problems, and Teddy O'Fines was nothing special. She didn't have to worry about shoplifting at the Home the way she used to worry that she would be caught. She had nowhere to go.

Whee was walking around the tables kissing everyone now, her eyes red from all the crying she'd been doing in the last weeks as her wedding day approached, her smile broad, lipstick on her white, white teeth.

Teddy cringed. Everything about the evening was beginning to feel artificial. And Whee — perfect, brilliant, beautiful Whee — was smiling and kissing through her tears, as if this night was her last free night before she was locked in prison until *"death did part her and Victor Treat."*

Danny was getting up to give his toast, a little drunk. Danny was often a little drunk, not every night but every party, and there had been a lot of parties in preparation for Whee and Victor's wedding. Teddy, sequestered in the Home for Girls with Problems, had not attended these parties, but Jess had and wrote to her about them.

Hi Teddy, was the note Teddy kept under her pillow. *Thinking about you all the time day and night while Whee Whee is the center of the universe, party after party, last night at the Gordons. Cocktails. They asked me did I want a Shirley Temple. If I'd been YOU, I would have said, "No, thanks, I actually drink champagne." But I'm not brave enough to be you, so I just said, "No, thank you."*

You are my idol. You have always been my idol because you tell the truth.

Love forever and ever and ever and ever, Jess, the save-the-marriage baby.

Danny raised his hands for quiet.

"Hello," he said. "Welcome, everyone, to the celebration of my beloved sister Louisa's marriage to Victor Treat." He raised his glass of champagne and drank. "To the two of you. Good luck, Victor, my friend, the brother I've never had. Welcome to the O'Fines family — we're a high-spirited, noisy, joyful, outspoken family, and We Love You!"

"I don't love him," Teddy said to her father, who was resting his chin in his hand, a thoughtful expression on his face. "Do you?"

Aldie gave Teddy a wink.

"Love him? Sure. He's about to be family."

"He isn't family yet," Teddy said, folding her legs under her, light-headed. Maybe she would faint.

She had never fainted before and it was possible she would now, tonight, in the Bay Room of the Brambles Hotel. She tried to concentrate on her father as he poured himself a glass of wine.

"What is family anyway?" Teddy asked.

"Family? Well, family is what we have."

"I mean, what is *our* family?" she asked. "As opposed to other families."

"Our family is like most families. A lot of good times. Loving and loyal. And a couple of problems."

"You mean me, I suppose."

He put his finger to his lips.

"Shhh. Danny's speaking."

"I wish you the happiness that Beet and I have," Danny was saying, "and the joy of a baby like our Ruby, who at this very moment is in the care of the best little sister in the world. A toast to Jess O'Fines, to the future, and to the loyalty of a loving family."

"Oh my god," Teddy said. "I am certainly going to throw up now."

"Get a grip," Delilah said.

Delilah's hot breath was windy in Teddy's ear with the sweet smell of champagne, and Teddy could feel the coming of an attack. A familiar tightness in her throat, her face damp, her heart beating so hard it felt as if it could jump out of her chest.

She had to get out of the room quickly, without causing a fuss or throwing up between her chair and the exit door, without losing her heart, which was about to burst through her skin and drop in a free fall from her body to the floor.

This was a *panic attack*. It had happened before. Three times in the last few months, once on the train home for Christmas. Out of the blue, she'd thought she was dying, and she'd gone into the bathroom and sat on the floor, concentrating on the whiteness of the toilet bowl until she began to feel like herself again. The other two times happened at the Home, and a counselor, Dr. Peach, very young, with wild curly hair, had held her by the wrists, speaking to Teddy in the softest voice she had ever heard.

"I promise you," she had said. "You are not going to die."

"But I can't catch my breath. I'm having a heart attack."

"You are not having a heart attack, Teddy. You are having a panic attack."

A panic attack.

"It happens," Dr. Peach had said. "Especially to girls, it happens. You are worried and nervous and uncertain, and out of the blue, like a locomotive hurrying down the tracks, you have this thing happen to you that feels like dying. But it isn't."

Dr. Peach had taught her how to breathe into a paper bag, in and out, in and out, so there was a balance of carbon dioxide and oxygen.

"Like this," she had said, showing Teddy what to do. And it did help and Teddy did feel better.

But now, in the Bay Room of the Brambles Hotel, at her sister's rehearsal dinner, sitting between her parents, Teddy O'Fines was not about to request a paper bag of the waitstaff.

She struggled to get up, pushing back the chair.

"I'll be right back," she said to her mother, breathing deeply to get more air into her lungs. "I'll bring the safety pin."

"Are you all right?" Delilah asked. "Do you want me to come with you?"

"No, no," Teddy said. "I'm fine."

"You look terribly pale." Delilah took her by the wrist.

"I'm fine," Teddy said, lifting up the chair. "I have to pee."

And she would be right back, she told herself. She'd go to the ladies' for a few minutes, where she would throw cold water on her face, sit on the toilet seat with the cubicle locked, taking in deep breaths, and then she'd go back to the rehearsal dinner.

Her tiny purse with a long ribbon hung over her shoulder, and as she was sitting, breathing, her eyes closed, she heard the *whoop* of a text message.

She opened the purse, checked the phone, and there it was, three words:

Help! Terrible trouble.

Jess.

Teddy got up quickly, opened the door, and ran out of the ladies', down the long corridor beyond the Bay Room, into the lobby, and over to the elevators, pushed UP, and waited as the doors creaked open.

She was alone in the elevator except for an elderly lady checking her lipstick in the mirror and in the mood for conversation.

"A very lovely hotel," she said, and Teddy nodded.

"I'm always happy to be at a lovely hotel, aren't you?" She smiled.

Teddy nodded.

The 2 was lit in the panel above the elevator doors, but they were moving very slowly. Four more floors to go.

"I'm here for my niece's wedding. My great-niece, actually, Miranda duFall. Do you know her?"

"I don't," Teddy said, as the doors opened on six.

"Well, have a nice day, now," the elderly lady said.

A Nice Day?

A member of the cleaning staff was standing at the door to room 618 with a pile of towels.

"You live here?" she asked Teddy with an accent, maybe French, maybe not.

Teddy nodded.

"Well, nobody's here and the door's open. I've been waiting for the folks to come back." She shrugged her shoulders.

"Nobody's here?"

Teddy stepped over the threshold.

The Pack and Play was set up, a towel spread out on the floor, and on the bed, tossed there, the skirt brushing the carpet, was Whee's wedding dress — draped casually across the bed, as if someone had been wearing it and suddenly had to leave in a hurry but without the dress.

"You the bride?" the cleaning lady asked.

"No," Teddy said.

She picked up the dress, Whee's precious and expensive wedding dress. She hung it up on the shower bar in the bathroom.

Whee's makeup was scattered on the sink.

***

So Jess had been in the bathroom, probably feeling sorry for herself, and a little angry, although she wasn't ever angry like Teddy, who was almost always a little angry. Jess must have looked at herself in the mirror and decided on a whim to try bronzer on her cheeks, sky-blue eye shadow, the raspberry lipstick that Whee must have purchased just for her wedding day.

Teddy dumped the tubes and brushes and pots back in the makeup bag, setting them on the side of the sink. She turned on the water to wash out the dusting of blue eye shadow.

Jess must have tried on the dress. Surprising, Teddy thought. Not like Jess to do something forbidden. By nature she wanted to please, to be admired and loved, to be helpful and cooperative, all of the good things that endeared her to her teachers and parents and her brother and sisters.

But Teddy suspected that Jess wasn't *really* obedient or dutiful or happy-go-lucky. She played the part of the good daughter in the O'Fines family the way Teddy played the part of the bad one.

"Well I'll be," the cleaning lady said, coming into the bathroom. "Some beautiful dress."

"It's my older sister's dress," Teddy said. "She gets married downstairs in this hotel tomorrow."

"Very nice for her."

"Have you seen my little sister, who was here in this room taking care of my baby niece when we left to go to the rehearsal dinner?"

"I've seen nothing except that dress. When I came on this floor to turn down the beds, the door was open."

"Not even a baby?"

"I heard a baby but I was working, so —" She hesitated. "Babies are all over the hotel, you know. I may have heard a baby, but it wasn't necessarily your baby."

She started to pull the door shut. "See you later," she said cheerfully. "I'll send your sister up here if I see her."

"Thanks," Teddy said, sitting down on the end of the bed.

She took her phone out of her purse.

WHAT is going on? she texted Jess. **I'm in the room.**

She waited. She waited and waited, counting to a hundred, counting to a thousand. No answer. No text returned.

Something was very much the matter.

CHAPTER FOUR

AN UNFORTUNATE DISCOVERY

Jess knew.

Standing beside the closed door wearing Whee's wedding dress, unzipped and too long with just the smallest amount of lipstick staining the inside of the top of the bodice — nothing to worry about, Jess hoped. But she simply *knew* that when she opened the door she would see the towel on the floor where she had left Baby Ruby before she went into the bathroom in the first place. And Baby Ruby would be gone.

She stood beside the door without opening it. Waiting. Waiting for Ruby to cry, waiting for Teddy to leave the rehearsal dinner and rush into room 618 to help her.

It felt like hours that Jess waited in the bathroom, and when finally she opened the door, the terry cloth towel was still spread out on the carpet, the door to 618 was closed, and there was no evidence that anyone had come into the room.

But Baby Ruby was gone.

Still in Whee's wedding dress, she rushed into the corridor of the hotel to check if the kidnapper was still there. She dashed toward the bank of elevators, but the hall was empty. She turned back to their room and crumpled to the floor, her heart beating in her chest so loud she could hear it, her brain scrambled eggs.

She pressed her face into the thick carpet, wishing to melt into the rug, wishing for an earthquake or fire or some great catastrophe to overtake the fact that Baby Ruby was gone.

Mainly, she wished that Teddy were there.

She reached for her cell phone on the end of the bed.

Help! Terrible trouble.

Teddy O'Fines had had experience with trouble. Real life-threatening trouble.

Just the thought of Teddy gave Jess the strength to get up from the floor.

The strength to take off Whee's wedding dress and toss it *carefully* on the bed, to slip into her shirt and jeans, push her cell phone into her back pocket, and hurry down the corridor in the direction of the elevators, where less than an hour ago she had seen the suspicious man.

She replayed what had happened. How odd the man had seemed standing by the bank of elevators as if he were going to get on an elevator. And then he didn't.

Jess had been in the doorway of room 618, holding Baby Ruby, when the man turned abruptly and headed in her direction. Alarmed, she stepped back into the room, shut the door, and put Baby Ruby on her back in the middle of the bed.

She opened the door again, just a crack, to check if he was still in the corridor, and the man was now in sunglasses. Just as she saw him, Baby Ruby began to scream. Had she closed the door when she rushed to pick her up?

Had she closed the door completely or not? Or had she been in too much of a hurry? Too distracted?

She had put Baby Ruby on the bed, spread a large white bath towel on the carpet, picked up Ruby, and put her on the towel on her back.

But had she actually *shut* the door? Or simply let it swing shut behind her while she picked up Ruby.

It was possible — she had to admit to herself — it had not been completely closed. She didn't test it to be certain it was locked.

The man certainly had seen *Jess*. He would also have seen Baby Ruby in her arms. He might have stopped at the door to room 618, waited, maybe even peered in if the door was not completely shut. Or perhaps the man had lurked in the hallway until Jess went into the bathroom. And then he had slipped into room 618, seen

Baby Ruby on the terry cloth towel, grabbed the baby, and left for nowhere.

Nowhere was how it felt.

A baby stolen from a room in a huge hotel could be anywhere in the hotel or out, in Los Angeles or beyond.

It had taken only a second to steal her, and then, maybe, there was a car waiting in the back of the hotel. The corridors were dark, the baby was wrapped in the man's jacket as he hurried down the exit steps. A leap into the car and Baby Ruby was gone, gone, gone.

The corridor was empty, but Jess could hear an elevator advancing — the light above the elevators indicated it was stopped at the fourth floor on its way up. Maybe it would stop at six and maybe — who could tell — someone in her family was in it. Maybe it was even Teddy escaping from the wedding, slipping out of the Bay Room to come help her sister.

Jess looked quickly around for a place to hide and, spotting the door just to the left of the elevators where she'd seen the housekeeper with a stack of towels, she opened it, slipped in, and left it open a crack.

A small room or a large closet, stacks of towels and sheets, boxes of soaps, shampoos, body cream. She closed the door behind her, edging her body between the sheets and towels, and listened to the sounds outside the door.

The elevator stopped, the doors opened, and then quick-stepping heels on the hardwood floor. A tall figure flashing by in the slit of the doorway, then silence as the footsteps faded away. It wasn't Teddy. Jess shut the door.

She leaned against the stack of starched sheets and closed her eyes. The room was almost dark, light coming under the door, but gradually her eyes adjusted to the darkness, to the silence of a room full of sweet-smelling linen. For the moment, she was invisible. She had to decide what to do. No time to wait.

She checked her phone. Five minutes. Only five minutes since she had first realized that Baby Ruby was gone, five very, very long minutes, and now she was sitting in the hotel linen closet.

Of course what she should do, what she *had* to do, was go down to the lobby and tell the person at the desk that her baby, Danny's baby but her responsibility for the night — Baby Ruby, of whom she was entirely in charge — had been stolen from room 618 while she tried on her sister's wedding dress in the bathroom with the door closed.

She leaned against the perfectly folded sheets and wished they would unfold and grab her in their starchy arms and swallow her up.

Then, just as she stretched out her legs, she felt the *whoop* in her back pocket where she had stuffed her cell phone.

WHAT is going on? Teddy texted. **I'm in the room.**

I'll be right there, Jess texted back.

She pushed herself up from the stack of sheets, her heart bubbling in her chest, rehearsing in her head what she would say to Teddy. Her sister was certainly the best member of her family to tell about this kind of trouble. Nevertheless, even if Teddy mostly hated the O'Fineses, and especially Danny, she was going to be horrified that her perfect little sister had lost the baby and ruined the family.

And that is how Jess saw it. Ruby had evaporated into thin air. The chances of finding her anywhere in this huge hotel were not good. And even if Ruby were found — poor Baby Ruby, counting on Jess to take care of her, to keep her from harm — what good would that do since Jess had been the one to lose her in the first place. She would never be forgiven. Not by Danny or Beet or even Aldie and Delilah, who would look at their youngest daughter as some kind of criminal.

They would never trust her again. They would never truly love her again. She would be better off in prison. Better off dead.

She opened the linen closet door, and there was a rustle behind her, the sound of breath, a presence or a ghost, and light crept into the dark room.

"What are you doing in here?"

A woman's voice, high and girlish, an accent, probably Spanish.

"Me?"

"You!"

Jess looked into the darkness in the direction of the voice, into the corner of the room, at a shadow of a woman, a small woman the size of a child, sitting on a short stack of sheets. She had long hair in braids hanging over her shoulders. Her feet were bare.

"You must leave," the woman said. "This room is for sheets and belongs to the hotel."

"I am leaving."

It struck Jess, a fly-by thought, floating in and then out of her mind, that the woman did not belong to the hotel either. So what was *she* doing in the linen closet?

"Good-bye," Jess said while closing the door. "I'm sorry to bother you."

There was no answer, no sound from the corner of the room, and when Jess crinkled her eyes, focusing on the spot where she had seen her, there was nothing. Only more white sheets.

～

Teddy was sitting on the edge of the bed, breathing into a paper bag, when Jess burst through the door.

"I had a full-on panic attack and now this." Teddy dropped the paper bag on the bed. "How in the world did Baby Ruby disappear?"

"She just did. Vanished! I was in the bathroom —"

"I *know* you were in the bathroom trying on Whee's wedding dress —"

"I was only in the bathroom for a second, Teddy."

"Long enough to also dump Whee's makeup. And look at you, lipstick, mascara, blush. Jeez, Jess."

"I want to die," Jess said through her tears.

"You *can't* die until we find Ruby."

They ran down the hall to the elevators, pressed the button, and stepped inside.

"But we're not going to ruin the rehearsal dinner, Teddy."

"You mean not tell Mom and Dad?"

"Or Danny and Beet."

"Or anyone in the family?"

"We're going to find Baby Ruby by ourselves," Jess said.

Her heart was still hammering away in her chest, but she had stopped crying. There was still a chance they could find Baby Ruby somewhere in the huge hotel or even Los Angeles.

"Remember SLEUTH, Jess?" Teddy said softly, looping her arm through her sister's, punching the LOBBY button of the elevator.

Jess nodded.

"It's going to come in handy now."

"So you agree, we'll find Ruby ourselves."

"We'll tell the concierge what has happened because we have to, and then we'll find her ourselves," Teddy said. "We're certainly very experienced with crime."

CHAPTER FIVE

THE GAME OF SLEUTH

The game of SLEUTH just happened out of the blue the night the O'Fineses announced that they were getting a divorce. When the conversation with their parents — not a conversation exactly, since what little Aldie and Delilah had to say had been cut short by Danny — was finally over, Aldie and Delilah left for the Woody Allen film, and the O'Fines children scattered. Teddy went upstairs to her bedroom and Danny headed out the front door with Whee. *Lots of luck on ever seeing me again,* he called, the last to leave, slamming the door behind him. Jess waited until Danny's car pulled out of the driveway and then went upstairs to Teddy's room.

The door was locked.

"Teddy?"

"Teddy O'Fines doesn't live here any longer."

"That's okay," Jess said, sitting on the floor and leaning against the door to Teddy's room. "I can wait until she comes back."

She waited, occasionally pressing her ear to the door, but there was no sound from Teddy's room. And then she heard shuffling, a window closing, bare feet slapping the hardwood floor.

"So come on in," Teddy said when she opened the door. "I'm sleeping. I'm planning to sleep for the rest of my life."

"I want to sleep too," Jess said. "With you."

"No problem," Teddy said. "Just stick to your side of the bed."

"Tonight has been a very bad night so far."

"It's not going to get any better, so crawl in, get under the covers, and tell me a story."

Jess lay very quietly next to her sister, her favorite sister. Tonight, this terrible night, which felt as if it were the end of her childhood, Teddy was the only person in the O'Fines family she truly loved.

"Did you know this was going to happen?" she asked.

"Sort of. I saw signs."

"Like what?"

"Like Daddy didn't sleep with Mom any longer. He slept on the couch in the TV room."

"I thought he was working late."

"Every night?"

"He's a very busy lawyer. That's what he told me. *I'm a very busy lawyer, Jess, and I need to stay up late to work.* Like that, he told me."

"He may be a very busy lawyer, but that's not why he was sleeping on the couch," Teddy said. "So tell me a story, Jess. A made-up story."

"Well." Jess propped up a pillow behind her.

"Like a fantasy story," Teddy said.

"This is a fantasy with us in it and it starts: *Once upon a time,* there were these two sisters, Jessica and Teddy O'Fines. Very pretty and very smart and they lived alone on Elm Street in Larchmont, New York, where their parents used to live until they decided to bolt, leaving them without any money to buy food or to pay the rent or to get Tylenol when they had a fever. So the sisters needed a job."

"What about school?"

"They didn't go to school. They didn't need to go to school because their parents weren't there to tell them what they could do or could not do. So one day while they were lying around in bed trying to decide whether to get an ice-cream sundae or go on a bike ride, they heard a terrible scream and Jess ran to the window to see what had happened and there in the backyard next to their old jungle gym was the body of a very fat woman lying facedown so all they could see was her blond hair and big bottom."

"Was she dead?"

"I don't know yet," Jess said. "Let's go to the window and check."

"You mean she's there in the backyard. Our backyard?"

"Of course."

Teddy followed Jess to the window above the back garden and they both looked down.

"She looks pretty dead, doesn't she?"

"I don't think she's breathing if that's what you mean," Teddy said, looking out the window at their dog, Chaucer, tearing up a basketball. "Chaucer is so very stupid that he doesn't even notice the fat woman on her stomach in our garden."

"Call the police, Ted," Jess said.

"Pronto," Teddy said, and she pretended to dial the police. 911.

"Come fast," she said. "There's a dead woman in the backyard of 301 Elm Street."

"Are they on their way?" Jess asked.

"Hear the sirens?"

The police came, two squad cars with their sirens whirring, parking outside the front of the house, and Teddy answered their knock.

"Glad to see you, gentlemen," she said, opening the door to the police. "My partner is in the back garden with the victim."

"Your partner?"

"My sister and I are partners in SLEUTH LLC. We'll be glad to help you out with this victim of some terrible crime. We are expert investigators."

And so SLEUTH LLC began that evening.

Jess and Teddy were in the back garden when Delilah got home from the movies.

"What's going on?" she called to them. "It's after nine."

"We're busy."

"Well, busy yourself into the house and get ready for bed."

"We're busy," Teddy called. "And afterward we'll go to bed."

Jess took on the role of the policeman.

"Ever see this woman before?" she asked.

"No, but then, I can't see her face," Teddy said.

"Any clues?" Jess asked.

"Well, she's a stranger and it looks as if she jumped from the second floor of our house, but as far as we know she was never in our house," Teddy said.

"No more clues?" Jess asked.

"Someone must have brought her here, someone very strong, strong enough to carry this victim and lay her facedown on our grass."

All summer, Jess and Teddy played SLEUTH, and in the fall after school started up again, they played most afternoons. A latchkey child now that Delilah had gotten a job in a bank, Jess would come home at three, let herself in the front door, walk Chaucer around the block, make herself a peanut-butter-and-cracker sandwich, and then set up a crime scene. A body might be hidden under their mother's bed, halfway under, just the feet showing. The drawers with Delilah's jewelry would be dumped on the carpet in the bedroom where Aldie O'Fines used to sleep in the bed with Delilah, and there'd be no other clues. Or the body of a man might be sitting on the chaise lounge where he'd been reading a book, the book in his lap, a bullet in the middle of his head leaving a bloody circle on his forehead.

During the fall semester Teddy had basketball, but after practice she would rush home and race up the steps to the second floor, where Jess had arranged a new crime scene.

The house was empty of men that year. Aldie was in the city, not even in Larchmont for weekends. The girls took turns going into the city to see him, but Whee was in her last year of college and Danny was a sophomore at Tufts, so only Teddy and Jess were in the house with Delilah.

It was the year of Delilah's First Boyfriend, and he would often call at the last moment to go out to dinner, so Delilah would leave the girls, her daughters — her precious daughters — to what she called *your own devices.*

"What is *devices*?" Jess had asked Teddy, sitting on the front porch swing while Teddy watched the eighth-grade boys pass the O'Fines house on their way to football practice.

"It means that we can do whatever we want to do. *Our own devices.*"

"Good," Jess said. "I *want* to do whatever I want to do. I just don't like Mom's boyfriend."

The game of SLEUTH filled the time until dinner, beef stew or chicken cacciatore Delilah had left bubbling in a slow cooker just in case her First Boyfriend called to take her out to dinner.

Jess described SLEUTH to her friends as a murder mystery game that always, by necessity, took place in their house on Elm Street. Terrible things happened that year in the O'Fines clapboard colonial, painted yellow with black shutters. But the criminal was almost always discovered, turned in to the police, and then incarcerated — justice was done, thanks to the O'Fines sisters.

Teddy and Jess, PRIVATE EYES.

Jess's favorite victim was Mrs. De Carlo, who had been Teddy's fourth-grade teacher and lived across the street with Mr. De Carlo and their cat, Alicia-kitty-kitty.

"You'll never guess what happened," Jess would say as Teddy hurried into the house from basketball. "Mrs. De Carlo is lying in Mom's room in a pool of blood."

"Knifed?" Teddy would ask, a look of gleeful alarm on her face.

"Undoubtedly," Jess would reply. "But I couldn't find the weapon."

Teddy would drop her backpack in the hall, grab a glass of milk and some sugar cookies from the jar in the kitchen, and follow Jess upstairs.

"Did you call the police?" Teddy asked.

"The police called me. They had a tip that Mrs. De Carlo was dead."

Jess opened the door to Delilah's room, where Mrs. De Carlo was lying on the floor. There was evidence of blood on the rug, fingerprints of blood on the four-poster bed where Delilah slept, on the recently painted yellow walls.

"Disgusting," Teddy said.

Catsup. They washed it off before Delilah came home from work.

They kept a bag of tools in the hall closet for fingerprints and blood samples and any other evidence around the body. Teddy crouched next to Mrs. De Carlo, took a tiny knife from her kit, and sliced off a sliver of skin from Mrs. De Carlo's finger.

"So what do you think happened?" Jess asked.

"I think Mrs. De Carlo came to our house to steal jewelry. Maybe Mom's old wedding ring."

"What makes you think that?"

"You see for yourself, Jess. Here she is deader than a doornail in Mom's room and the jewelry drawer is open, yes?"

Jess giggled.

"Of course," she said, always pleased when Teddy commented on her clues. "You're so smart."

"But I'm pretty sure Mr. De Carlo is the real culprit."

"How come Mr. De Carlo?"

"He may seem nice enough, sort of harmless," Teddy said on her knees, putting the blood on a glass slide. "But my guess is he's been thinking that life would be a lot easier without Mrs. De Carlo, and who can blame him."

"So he *told* her to steal the jewelry, right?"

"That's what I figure," Teddy said. "They don't have a lot of money and no responsibilities except Alicia-kitty-kitty, and he's been thinking maybe it would be nice to go to the Bahamas."

"Right, and where would he get the money?"

"Exactly," Teddy said.

"Mom looks a little rich and she's divorced and probably keeps her good jewelry in a box in her room. So he thinks to himself, *I'll go over while the kids are in school. Everyone knows Delilah O'Fines is not the type to lock her front door.*

"So in comes Mrs. De Carlo and she never even gets a chance to take anything of Mom's. Right behind her with his special knife is Mr. De Carlo, and slice, slice, slice . . ."

"She's dead."

"And he takes the jewelry and what do you bet he'll be in the Bahamas tonight."

"So should I call the police?" Jess asked.

"Pronto."

"Tell them our suspicions?"

"Tell them to send one man here to take Mrs. De Carlo to the morgue."

"And another officer to head for the airport and stop Mr. De Carlo."

"Perfect, Jess. That was waaaay too easy," Teddy said. "Now we've got to clean up the catsup on Mom's bedspread, unless the police have another case."

Which was how their afternoons went, one murder after another — movie stars, rock musicians, neighbors, all murdered in Delilah's bedroom or their father's old study, and once in the kitchen.

And then, sometime after Christmas that year, during the January sales at the shops in downtown Larchmont, Teddy O'Fines started to shoplift, and SLEUTH LLC was finished.

CHAPTER SIX

POLICE REPORT?

The elevator doors opened at the *L* level, and Teddy followed Jess out into the lobby, crowded with young women in shimmery, short dresses and strappy high heels, holding long-stem glasses of champagne. There was a live band and close dancing and a huge bunny made of ice with a top hat cocked between his ears, towering halfway to the ceiling.

"The concierge will tell us where to find the police," Teddy said, surprisingly calm. "And the police will find her."

It didn't occur to Teddy that something terrible might have happened to Baby Ruby. After all, they were in a hotel, plenty of people around to notice a baby, a crying baby, carried by a stranger. Ruby had probably been lying on the towel in room 618, crying and crying. Someone who worked at the hotel overheard her and had a key and had come in to check the room. Thinking the baby had been left alone, she picked her up and left for another part of the hotel.

"Jess," she said, taking a gentle hold of her little sister's wrist. "Didn't Ruby cry?"

"Nope," Jess said. "At least I didn't hear her crying."

Was the water running the whole time, and was that why she didn't hear Ruby?

"The police will find her safe and sound," Teddy said, leaning into her sister, feeling Jess's fear as if it had weight.

Jess could only imagine the worst.

Ruby would *never* be found. She had been taken from the hotel and out into the city of Los Angeles to somewhere else. Maybe she had been kidnapped by the small man she had seen outside the elevators.

Or Ruby was dead.

And Jess would be in prison.

Over and over in her mind's eye, Jess saw Baby Ruby lying on the towel on her back, her little legs dancing in the air.

She should *never* have shut the bathroom door to try on Whee's makeup. That was the second mistake. And when she rushed to pick up a crying Baby Ruby, she should have double-checked to be sure that the door was really locked.

Her stomach was in knots, her breath so thin she was dizzy walking with Teddy across the lobby. She needed huge gulps of air or it was possible she'd faint.

Dying is how it felt.

"What does dying feel like?" she asked Teddy. "You know, like when you have those panic attack things and you think you're dying?"

"No air is how it feels," Teddy said.

"I can't breathe."

"You're breathing," Teddy said, giving her a squeeze. "Just not deep enough."

"I keep thinking what I will tell the police."

"You'll tell them the truth, Jess," Teddy said. "They're supposed to help us out."

"Maybe."

"That's their job, to help people in trouble."

"Well, I'm a person in trouble."

If Jess told the police the truth, they would know it was her fault. *Why*, they'd ask her, was she was trying on her sister's wedding dress in the first place? If she was going to play dress-up, *why* didn't she leave the bathroom door open so she could still *see* Baby Ruby lying on the towel in room 618?

She wondered, would she be able to speak to the police at all?

Or would she bolt?

"Do you remember how long it was between the time you went into the bathroom and then discovered that Baby Ruby was missing?" Teddy asked. "The police will want to know that."

"Five minutes, maybe."

"It had to be more than five minutes, Jess. You're totally made-up. Lipstick, blush, that foundation stuff. Even mascara."

"Maybe ten minutes. Fifteen at the most," Jess said. "What're you going to ask the person when we get to the concierge desk?"

"I'll tell them we have a missing baby and could they contact the police."

"I have to pee first," Jess said, touching Teddy on the arm.

"No, stay," Teddy said. "This will just take a second and then you can pee."

But even before Teddy finished her sentence, Jess bolted.

In the cubicle, she locked the door and checked her phone.

Eight thirty. An hour and a half since her family had left on the elevator for the rehearsal dinner, since she had stood in the open doorway of room 618 and watched them go and seen the strange little man walking in her direction, taking her into account.

For a while she had chattered to Baby Ruby, maybe half an hour, maybe a little bit more, and then she went into the bathroom and opened the makeup bag with Whee's new stash. Seven thirty or seven forty-five.

Maybe fifteen minutes since she left the linen closet and met up with Teddy. And in all the time between, she had been in the bathroom.

She realized that she'd been in the bathroom of room 618 for as long as half an hour — half an hour with the door shut and the water running. She would not have been able to hear Baby Ruby if she cried. Her heart fell.

She fled the ladies' room, through the door and across the lobby, running in the direction of the elevators, looking for an exit sign.

She would not tell the police.

Somewhere in this hotel or in Los Angeles or on a plane or train or bus, Baby Ruby was still alive, and Jess would find her. She had lost her and she would find her.

Jess wasn't a babysitter any longer. She was a criminal.

Everywhere she went, Jess O'Fines was known as a *super* girl — in Larchmont, at her grandmother's house in New Haven, in New York City where her father lived. Not a goody-goody or a teacher's pet or even a girl who *never* got into trouble. She got into trouble, small trouble, failing a test, forgetting her homework or leaving her backpack at the market, or not going to bed at nine o'clock p.m. *flat* as Delilah insisted.

But she wasn't selfish or complaining or rude or unkind. For that matter, she wasn't afraid of consequences in the way that good girls are sometimes good only because they are afraid of what will happen if they aren't.

If Jess was unhappy, no one knew about it. Not even her mother and never Whee. Sometimes she told Teddy, but Teddy was living at the Home for Girls with Problems and could only talk to her family once a week.

Everyone thought of Jess as a girl who didn't let the problems in her life get her down.

She made mistakes but never big ones — not like Danny, who was irresponsible, or Teddy, who turned the family upside down by stealing, or even golden-girl Whee, sweet, successful Whee.

Delilah had even said that Whee won the Blue Ribbon in a character contest, First Place for Selfishness.

Jess kept the bad news to herself.

Now she had done something terribly wrong, worse than anyone in her family had ever done. She was certainly more of a serious criminal than Teddy, who had only stolen things. Stealing may be against the law, but no one had ever been hurt by Teddy's shoplifting except Teddy herself.

Jess opened the exit door next to the elevators, which led to the stairs, and sat down on the bottom step, dialing Teddy.

"Jess!"

"I am not going to tell the police."

"You have to tell them," Teddy said.

"This is my fault. It's what I'm doing, Ted, and I need you to help me."

"It's crazy," Teddy said. "It may even be against the law not to report what happened to the police. We're losing valuable time, Jess."

"The police would ask me all these questions and fill out their reports, and by the time they'd finished, Baby Ruby could be on an airplane for Guatemala and we'd never see her again."

"Where are you?"

"I'm here," Jess said. "Go to the elevators, the ones we just got off, and next to them is a door with an exit sign above it. Open the door and I'm sitting on the bottom step."

~

It was the previous winter, especially cold and snowy in Larchmont for March. Jess, just home from school on a Thursday afternoon, had been in the kitchen standing at the fridge. She was examining the slim contents of the shelves for a snack when the telephone call came from the police to report that Teddy had shoplifted at the jewelry counter at Saks Fifth Avenue. She was at the store in the office on the fourth floor, waiting to be picked up by an adult. She had been charged.

Delilah had answered the phone.

"Oh god, no," Delilah said.

Jess took a strawberry yogurt, closed the door to the fridge, and slid into a kitchen chair.

"Charged?" Delilah said. "Yes, of course."

Tears were streaming down her cheeks.

"Charged. I understand. Of course."

She hung up the phone and leaned against the stove.

"I have to go to the city," she said, sinking into a chair. "Saks. I haven't a clue where to park in the city."

"Is everything going to be okay?" Jess asked.

"No, it's not going to be okay at all," Delilah said, standing.

She put on her trench coat, checking her face in the mirror in the hall.

"No one's injured or dead, but Teddy lifted a diamond bracelet at Saks this afternoon."

She brushed the tears off her face with the sleeve of her coat.

Jess was standing now, putting on her jacket, slipping her backpack over her shoulders.

"So this means she skipped afternoon classes, took the train to New York, headed uptown to Saks, and . . ." Delilah didn't finish her sentence.

"I want to come with you to New York," Jess said.

"No, Jess," Delilah said. "You are not coming with me." She leaned down and rested her cheek against Jess's. "You, my one good-as-gold child, are going across the street to the Grosses' and I'll call from the city to let you know what's up. Do your homework."

"I *need* to come with you."

"You don't, Jess. You need to do your homework and not spend the afternoon on the phone."

Jess folded her arms across her chest.

"I'm going up to get my purse and keys and heading out pronto. So you decide, babe, it's here or the Grosses'. Let me know."

Jess had decided.

With her mother upstairs, she slipped out the front door, opened the door to the gray minivan in the driveway, crawled into the far backseat, and pulled the blanket used for Chaucer over her whole body and head.

"Bye, babes," she could hear her mother call to her as she opened the car door and climbed in, turned on the engine. Jess could tell she was backing out of the drive onto Elm Street.

Even before Delilah had turned off Elm Street onto the highway, she was on the phone. First to Mrs. Gross.

"I'm on my way to the city for a minor emergency, Patty, and have left Jess alone to do her homework, so I'm checking to see if she can call you if she needs help."

And then she called Aldie about Teddy.

"I cannot handle her, Aldie. You're in the city. Maybe we could meet at Saks."

There was a pause, but Jess could not hear her father's voice.

"I think she should live with you for the rest of the year and go to P.S. 101 or wherever. I have no effect whatever on her. She cannot even hear my voice."

The blanket smelled of dog, so Jess took it off her head and kept her head behind the row of seats, where her mother couldn't see her.

Teddy would want her there. Jess was sure of it. She needed to be there, just in case the police suggested that Teddy go to jail. Or *insisted* that she go to jail. Jess would go to jail with her. Just the thought of jail with Teddy, closed up in a little cell with her sister and no parents, only a police guard outside their room, had an appeal to Jess. That close to her sister, Teddy's protector, her very best friend.

The ride was longer, much longer than it had seemed to Jess when she was sitting up in her seat and driving into the city. Delilah put on music and changed the station to news and then to NPR and then off.

"I'm so nervous," she said more than once, as if someone were in the car sitting next to her. The phone rang and she answered on the fifth ring. It was Aldie.

"Meet me in the office of Saks on the fourth floor," she said. "Be there."

Maybe Aldie responded and maybe he didn't, but Delilah was silent from that moment until the car stopped in the city. Delilah climbed out, and Jess sat up in the backseat.

Delilah said nothing. Nothing at all. Jess got out. Delilah locked the car, headed up the steps from the parking garage to the street and across Fifth Avenue, Jess following behind her. Through the doors of Saks Fifth Avenue, past the cosmetics and accessories to the other side of the store and the bank of elevators. In the elevator, Delilah didn't speak. Neither did Jess until the doors opened and they snaked through the counters of children's and teen's clothing to the office.

"I thought it would make Teddy happy to see me," she said finally.

"I'm sure it will," Delilah said.

"And I thought it might help you."

"That's a stretch," Delilah said. "What would help me is for my children, my beloved and impossible children, to do what I ask them to do."

Teddy was sitting in the middle of a long bench pushed against a wall in the main room of the office, a woman behind the counter on the telephone. A policeman leaning against the counter, waiting for her to get off the phone.

She was wearing dark pants, a green blouse that Jess knew she had shoplifted from Hudson's Department Store, and a navy basketball letter jacket with *L* in red on the back, which had belonged to Danny. She was facing forward, very still — her expression fixed, neither sad, nor combative, nor anything particular.

Her eyes met Jess's eyes, but she didn't smile.

Jess sat down beside her sister, conscious of the space between them, moving closer, leaning into her until their bodies touched.

At first, Teddy was a statue, immobile except for rolling the end of her green blouse into a long tube, concentrating on it. But gradually her body gave, and she pressed it into Jess's, slipped her hand between their hips where Jess's hand was locked, and held it.

"Thank you for coming, Jess," Teddy said under her breath.

Teddy opened the door under the exit sign and sat down on the step next to Jess.

"You haven't changed your mind about the police?"

"I haven't," Jess said.

"Mom and Dad? Danny? We need to tell them, Jess."

"I think you should go back to the rehearsal dinner and check it out, see what is happening, tell Mom you feel too sick to be there. We can't tell them yet. It will *RUIN* Whee's whole wedding."

"We have to," Teddy said. "We're losing time."

"Please, Teddy, give me one chance to check the linen closet where I saw this woman with long braids who looked as if she were hiding and see if she's still there. I just have this feeling I'll find out something."

"No, Jess."

"I'm going to do it. It's weird to find a woman who doesn't seem to work for the hotel hiding in the hotel's linen closet. You have to agree that it's weird! Please!"

"Okay, I'll go tell Mom, you check the linen closet, but only if you promise to tell an adult what's happened RIGHT afterward. Five minutes. No more, Jess. Promise."

"I promise. I totally promise I'll tell an adult," Jess said, breathless, her heart throbbing in her throat.

CHAPTER SEVEN

AN UNUSUAL CLUE

Jess got off the elevator, walked down the corridor to the end, and turned left. Room 618 was halfway down the hall, and there appeared to be a flurry of activity just outside their room.

Maybe, Jess thought, she should go back to the lobby, leave the hotel by the rear entrance facing the water, walk the path from the hotel to the Pacific Ocean. And swim to China.

But she kept walking.

The door to their room was open, and in the hall, three women wearing the hotel's grass-green uniforms were speaking Spanish too fast for Jess to understand, although she was in her second year of Spanish at school. They stopped talking when Jess arrived and then smiled and said, "Hello, hello, lady."

Inside the room, another woman in uniform was sitting on the bed. Whee's wedding dress was no longer there.

"Have you seen a dress that I left on the bed?" Jess asked the woman, who was sitting there as if the room were hers.

"In the bathroom," the woman said.

"And cleaned up the makeup that I left in the sink?" Jess asked, hoping her voice sounded as calm and normal as it did in her ear.

"It was already cleaned up."

The woman had turned toward the corridor, hushing the chattering women gathered there.

"Thank you."

Jess headed into the bathroom. She needed a moment to think. Just a moment. She had promised Teddy. She shut the door behind her, put the seat of the toilet down, and sat. Checking her cell phone — nine forty-five — she guessed the rehearsal dinner would be over in two hours just as Danny had said.

Outside the bathroom, she heard a din of voices, as if more people had arrived. Certainly the word was out among the staff, and she guessed they were all talking.

Ruby had disappeared a little more than an hour ago, but Jess couldn't allow herself to think that she was lost for good. She needed *hope*, and then she would have the energy to search and search and search. It was unlikely that one twelve-year-old girl with some experience as a detective, but not enough, could do this job alone.

But with Teddy's help, Jess would find her.

The door to the room was still open when Jess came out of the bathroom. The group was larger now and included the woman who had been sitting on the bed. They watched Jess as she walked out the door and shut it behind her.

"See you later," she said, sidestepping the group, all women and one man holding a broom, resting his chin on the handle.

"So sorry about the trouble," one of the women with a heavy accent said, and the others muttered in sympathy.

How did they know? she wondered. Had Teddy said something to them, had she asked where Baby Ruby was?

Certainly no one else in the O'Fines family could have heard.

She headed down the corridor to the linen closet.

~

Teddy hurried across the lobby to the rehearsal dinner, checking her phone.

No text from Jess yet. Five minutes, almost six had passed.

"Where have you been?" Delilah asked when Teddy sat down. "I went to the bathroom to look for you and you were gone."

"I went upstairs to the room to lie down."

"Is everything okay up there?" Delilah asked.

"Everything's fine. I had a panic attack and threw up, but otherwise

I'm great," she said, a little breathless. "So I'm going back up but I just wanted to tell you. Tell Whee I'm really sorry."

"You've been watching TV. I can tell. At your sister's rehearsal dinner."

"Leave her alone, Delilah," Aldie said. "If she doesn't feel well, then she doesn't feel well. Button up."

"Button up?" Delilah began, but Beet had gotten up and was walking toward them.

"Here comes Beet," Teddy said.

Everyone in the O'Fines family was a little afraid of Beet, tall and thin as a string bean, with long, thready brown hair.

She leaned over the table.

"Everything okay upstairs, Ted?" she asked.

"Everything's good," Teddy said. "At least it was when I left to come back downstairs."

"Baby Ruby sleeping?"

"Yes, sleeping."

"Cool," Beet said. "That's all I needed to know."

And she slithered her long body back to her table, ruffled Danny's hair, and gave him a kiss on the top of his head.

"I'll try to come back to the dinner before it's over," Teddy told her mother, "but not likely." And she slipped out the side door to the room.

She was heading toward the elevators when she heard a *whoop*.

Jess!

Meet me in our room. I think I have a clue.

z

The linen closet was dark. The tiny woman would certainly have gone by now, but Jess noticed a smell. She reached along the wall for a switch to turn on the light and the room lit up. No one was there, not even a trace that someone had been there except a depression in the stack of sheets where the woman had been sitting. She checked around the sheets to see if there was something the woman might have left, something to identify her. But there was nothing that Jess could find, even lifting up the sheets and running her hands along the cracks between them.

There *was* a smell: something sweet and familiar that didn't come from the sheets, which actually smelled of Clorox.

She took her cell out of her pocket and texted Teddy.

Meet me in our room. I think I have a clue.

Maybe Teddy would be able to identify the smell.

Something suspicious about the woman tucked away in the corner of the linen closet like a discarded rag doll.

And now, this smell.

Jess wasn't sure what it was, but it could be a clue to who she was and why she was hiding in the linen closet.

She walked around the rest of the sixth floor, which was almost too quiet for a Friday night. But as she walked by room 645, she heard the familiar sound of a baby's cry.

A baby's cry. What she had been listening to hear. Some possibility that Ruby was just down the hall in another room.

Jess knocked.

A woman in a pink flowered robe came to the door.

"Yes?"

"I just heard a crying baby," Jess said.

"You are looking for a baby?"

"Well, more or less."

"Is my baby keeping you up?"

The woman was not in a good humor.

"I haven't gone to bed," Jess said.

The woman started to shut the door but changed her mind and stepped out of the room, speaking quietly.

"Are you telling me you've *lost* a baby?"

"Temporarily," Jess said. "No problem, really."

"Temporarily? Temporarily you've lost a baby. Is that what you're telling me? Are you the babysitter?"

"The baby is not lost," Jess said quickly. "And I am not the baby-sitter. I'm the aunt."

"Well, I'm glad to hear that," the woman said and went back in her room.

~

For as long as Jess could remember, she had been sensitive to smells.

"You're like a dog, Jess," Delilah had said to her. "Sniffing and sniffing. I never knew a child with such a nose."

But she wasn't like a dog at all. Dogs sniffed for food and evidence of other animals, especially other dogs. Jess sniffed for memory.

She remembered places for how they smelled. Her grandmother's house in New Haven smelled of sugar cookies baking, and her uncle Tom's house smelled of ginger. Delilah smelled of Calvin Klein Eternity toilet water, and her father's apartment smelled of fried bacon. Her junior high school smelled of Lysol, and the Grosses' house smelled of gas. Standing on the sidewalk in front of their house, Jess always smelled gas.

So if she smelled sugar cookies, she thought of her grandmother, and if ginger, she had a picture of Uncle Tom, and even the kitchen of her own house smelled of Eternity toilet water, whether Delilah was in the kitchen cooking or not.

The smell in the linen closet of the sixth floor was distinct and familiar, but she could not name it.

"No luck?" a cleaning woman asked Jess as she came back to room 618.

"Not so far," Jess said.

The woman shrugged a weary shrug, as if she somehow had access to information that Baby Ruby would never be found.

"Too bad," she said.

Room 618 still smelled of Baby Ruby. The lingering smell of warm milk. The smell of spit-up and poop and baby powder.

There was a knock, the door opened, and Jess's heart leapt up.

Teddy was not a hugger, too cool to be a hugger, but she hugged Jess hard.

Jess could feel the tears in the back of her throat. She took a deep breath all the way down to her belly. If she started to cry, the tears would never stop.

"A clue?"

"Maybe it's a clue," Jess said. "It's a smell."

"Oh, Jess, you and your crazy smells."

"Follow me," Jess said, and they left the room, passing the cleaning ladies in the hall, and went down the corridor to the linen closet.

She opened the door, turned on the light, and Teddy followed her to the corner where the tiny woman had been sitting.

"She had long braids, so long they looped, and she was sitting on a stack of sheets and her feet didn't even touch the floor. It wasn't normal."

"What do you mean not normal?"

"She seemed to be hiding in the sheets and she certainly didn't want me to be there."

Jess bent down and touched the depression in the sheets where the woman had been sitting.

"There," she said. "See that dent in the sheets?"

"Sort of," Teddy said.

"Well, it's kind of a hole that was left since she was all scrunched up so no one could see her. But I could see her. Now smell the sheets."

Teddy leaned over and sniffed.

"Rosemary."

"Rosemary?"

"Christmas, remember? When Mom fills the dinner table with rosemary wreaths."

Jess leaned down and smelled the sheets again.

"You're right," she said.

"But a smell isn't going to be a clue to anything unless the woman reappears smelling of rosemary. And what difference would that make? You'd recognize her anyway. So now we're out of here and going to tell the concierge about Baby Ruby. As you promised."

"Okay," Jess said. "But remember, everything makes a difference when you're trying to solve a crime." And she turned off the light.

As she left the linen closet, a man rushed past.

Jess slipped into the corridor with Teddy behind her just as the doors to the elevator were closing. But she was not too late to see the man she recognized, the same man she had seen earlier walking down the corridor toward room 618 when she had backed into the room with Baby Ruby.

CHAPTER EIGHT

A SENSE OF SMELL

He had seen her.

He was looking at Jess when she walked out of the linen closet.

They had made eye contact.

Quickly, Jess lowered her eyes and slung her arm around Teddy's shoulder.

"Let's go," she whispered.

"Where're we going?" Teddy asked.

Jess checked the direction of the elevator. Headed down. She pushed the DOWN arrow.

"The man I told you about who was standing at the elevators when you and Whee were on your way to the rehearsal dinner?"

"The little guy in the green shirt."

"That one — I'm sure he saw me with Baby Ruby and headed in my direction and I stepped back into the room and shut the door."

The elevator opened and Teddy followed Jess inside.

"Or maybe I shut the door."

"I remember."

"I just saw him going to the elevator and he saw me."

"He recognized you?"

"I was standing outside the door to our room with Baby Ruby."

"But how do you know he recognized you just now?"

"Our eyes met. He knew it was me."

"So what are you thinking?"

"I'm thinking I didn't shut the door to the room all the way. That I just pulled it almost shut and I put Ruby on the floor, and I went in the bathroom and shut *that* door, and he stood outside room 618 and pushed the door and it opened."

"And you think he took Baby Ruby?"

"That's what I think."

"Honestly, Jess. You have a wild imagination."

The elevator doors opened onto a lobby crowded with people. Jess saw the collar of the green shirt winding its way through the crowd and she followed it. Teddy followed her past the concierge's desk and the information desk, past the girls in their party dresses. He was still in front of them, breaking free of the crowd, hurrying down a long corridor, and then he dropped out of sight.

Jess thought she saw him turn left, just ahead, a half a corridor ahead, but she couldn't be sure because it happened so fast.

"This is insane," Teddy was saying, hurrying to keep up.

"It's not insane, I promise." Jess came to the place where she lost sight of the green shirt, an exit sign above a door that opened to narrow stairs. She ran down the stairs, Teddy behind her. Down and down and down. Three floors down and then Jess saw him. He rushed through a door that shut behind him. By the time Jess got to the door, which was heavy, and pulled it open, he was a splash of green in the distance, running through the garage, in and out of the lines of parked cars.

Then they lost him.

"He's getting in his car," Jess said.

They'd stopped now, standing amidst the cars in a garage empty of people as far as they could tell.

"Duh!"

"Why would he run away from us unless he knows where Ruby is?"

"I don't know why, Jess," Teddy said. "Maybe he has to pee."

"This isn't funny," Jess said. "He has Baby Ruby somewhere, maybe in the car, and he's headed on his way out of here to Los Angeles or some other town. Follow me."

In the distance, but not that far away, they heard a car starting up.

"I don't want to follow," Teddy said. "We could be killed."

Jess didn't stop. She followed the sound of the engine starting up, winding through the cars. Two lanes away, a blue boxy car — she didn't know the names of cars but this was bright blue and square — was pulling out of its parking space, and she hurried in that direction.

"Jess," Teddy called. She was no longer following. "This is very stupid. We need the police."

"I know what I'm doing."

"You don't. This is real. It isn't SLEUTH."

But Jess was on a tear. She slid between a bank of cars, coming out into the open just as the blue car headed straight out of the garage, and she caught a glimpse of the green shirt, of the top of the man's head. *A blue box car,* she'd tell the police later, but the man was driving fast, too fast to be driving in the garage, and when Teddy called *Get his license number,* he was already too far away from Jess for the license plate to be anything but a blur.

"We have to tell the police, Jess. Now, while there is a chance of catching him."

Jess was out of breath.

"I'll tell them," Teddy said. "A bright blue, overweight car built in a square."

"I really don't want to talk to the police," Jess said.

"That's why I'll talk to them."

Teddy opened the door that led from the garage upstairs to the hotel.

"I thought I was the gutsy one between the two of us. But turns out you're the gutsy one and I'm just a regular run-of-the-mill kleptomaniac."

Behind her, Jess was crying. She couldn't help herself.

It was ten thirty on the clock over the main desk in the lobby when Jess and Teddy walked by, Teddy on her way to the information desk.

"Are you going to mention Baby Ruby?" Jess asked. "Please, not yet."

"We're both going to tell what's happened to Ruby. You know that."

"I can't," Jess said, leaning against a wall next to the ladies' room. "I'll wait for you here."

Jess closed her eyes. She had a funny feeling in her body, as if her insides were quivering, her kidneys and liver and intestines, the organs she'd studied in life sciences that year. She couldn't stop the shaking.

Teddy had taught her about deep breaths, and she tried it now.

Swallow the breath deep in your belly, hold it, breathe out slowly.

When she opened her eyes, there, just a short distance away, was her brother, Danny, his arm around Beet, talking to Delilah. They were headed in the direction of the elevators.

Jess slipped quickly into the ladies' room, opened a cubicle, locked it, and sat on the toilet with her feet up.

Just in time.

She heard the door open and Beet's loud and raspy voice.

"Danny and I are going to the bar to have a drink before we go upstairs," Beet was saying.

Jess heard a cubicle shut, the lock click — her heart beat in her mouth.

"I'm going up to the room now. I'm dead tired and a little woozy from the wine."

It was Delilah.

"I'll check on Ruby, Beet, and see you in the morning."

"Great party, Delilah," Beet said. "I had a blast."

Jess pressed her eyes into her knees, her hands hard against her ears so she could hardly hear anything but the beating of her own heart.

She didn't move at all. Her feet were on the toilet seat, her back against the tile wall, her legs bent, her forehead resting on her knees. Someone else from the rehearsal dinner was bound to come in, and so she waited.

What terrified Jess was that soon, any moment now, her mother would walk into room 618.

"Hello, hello," she'd call in a raspy singsong voice as she walked into their hotel room.

And no one would be there. Not the baby nor Jess nor Teddy.

Then what?

Delilah would go crazy.

She would rush downstairs to the bar to get Danny and Beet, who would fly upstairs to find there was NO BABY.

Maybe the woman smelling of rosemary had nothing to do with Baby Ruby. Maybe she had other reasons to hide, or maybe she and the man in the green shirt were together.

Whatever was going on or would go on, Jess was stuck in the fourth cubicle of the ladies' room, waiting for time to pass, for Teddy to come in and find her.

Waiting for other guests at Whee's rehearsal dinner to arrive and chat back and forth at the long sink.

~

Jess discovered her special sense of smell when she was very young. She smelled the air, which always had the scent of flavored water — mint water or strawberry water or cherry water. The air everywhere smelled of something, and Jess was aware of it. The air in the ladies' room at the hotel smelled of gardenias, so thick and sickly sweet that she wished the smell could be mixed with the smell of lemons to eliminate the sweetness. The air in Larchmont, especially in the spring and after a long rain, smelled of mold. Sort of like rats, she told her mother.

"We don't have rats," Delilah said, "so how can the air smell of rats if we don't have them? Or mold. Something is the matter with your nose, Jess, and maybe you need surgery."

"Larchmont smells moldy," Jess said. "All the time, even in winter."

"Well, why don't you keep what you're smelling to yourself," her father said. "It ruins my dinner."

And Jess did, most of the time, but that didn't stop her from smelling something in the air every place she went. Even her pediatrician's office, which was supposed to be the purest air of all.

But when SLEUTH LLC started, Jess's sense of smell turned out to be important to her work as a detective.

She could tell if Delilah had been in the bedroom that day or whether Miss Sally, who did the sheets and towels and smelled of Good Cheer detergent, had been there. She could tell if the air in the house had a new smell, maybe cucumber or stale vegetables or mint, which would indicate either that there had been a visitor or that the criminal of the day had taken a shower in mint gel.

Part of the excitement in discovering a crime had to do with smell, imaginary or real, and even Teddy loved that part of the game.

Jess had a sniffer, and Teddy had a brain. They were a perfect team of sleuths. At least that's the way Teddy described it to Jess.

The ladies' room filled up; maybe three or four women came in as a group and went into cubicles and locked the doors, talking back and forth, so they must have been at the same party.

"Did you hear about the baby?" a woman said.

"I didn't," another replied.

"What happened?"

"A baby seems to have disappeared. I overheard it in the elevator."

"No kidding," the second woman replied. "From where?"

"The hotel. I don't know what floor," the first woman said. "Just that the cleaning staff got wind of it."

"Awful!"

"Yup."

"In any case, the baby is gone and the hotel will probably be turned upside down searching for it, which is going to be a nightmare."

Jess covered her ears.

If these ladies had heard about Baby Ruby, maybe from the cleaning staff standing outside room 618, it was possible the police had already been called in, and maybe the O'Fines family had been notified.

Teddy had been gone for a long time. Too long. She checked her phone, and as she picked it up, there was a *whoop.*

> **Where are you?**
>
> **In the ladies next to the elevators on the first floor. Bad news.**
>
> **People know what happened.**

Whoop.

> **I'm coming exactly now.**

Jess dropped one shoe on the floor and pushed it under the door so it would be visible to Teddy when she walked into the ladies'. She unlocked the door.

Teddy saw the shoe, opened the door, and slipped carefully into the small space where Jess was sitting on the toilet seat, her face pale and stricken.

Teddy leaned down, picked up the shoe, and dropped it in Jess's lap.

"Are you okay?" she whispered in Jess's ear.

Jess nodded.

"They know at information."

"About the car?"

"No. They know about Baby Ruby. One of the cleaning ladies on our floor reported it."

"How did she know?"

"Either she overheard us or she guessed when I came into the room and found the dress and asked about you and Baby Ruby."

"Oh, jeez."

"And, Jess, the police have been called. The hotel reported that she was gone when I told them what had happened."

The women were still chatting back and forth, but the subject had changed to makeup and who wore blush and who used foundation and who was going to have an eyebrow lift like Fanny Burney in *Rising Stars* had done.

"We're going to make a run for it," Teddy said. "I'll go first and meet you in the corner by the plant where the elevators are. Count to one hundred and then go."

Jess waited to one hundred, and then she left, walking with a bouncy step so she would look confident and not at all the criminal that she was.

Teddy was waiting.

"Where now?" Jess asked.

"Now is our problem."

CHAPTER NINE

DIVIDE AND CONQUER

"We're kind of stuck," Jess said. They had gone out the back door of the hotel and stood in the dark next to one of the pillars on the porch.

"If stuck means we don't have a plan, we are stuck," Teddy said.

Jess rested her head against the pillar.

"I'm actually scared, Teddy."

"Me too."

"The guy in the green shirt was up to something or he wouldn't have raced away from us," Jess said.

"And what do you think about the woman smelling of rosemary?" Teddy asked.

"She was weird," Jess said. "Kind of a girl-woman with long braids, stuffed into the corner of the hotel linen closet. Something was wrong."

In the game of SLEUTH, Jess and Teddy followed clues. They kept a list. They wrote down the facts exactly as they imagined them.

Description of suspect. Color of hair and eyes and clothes. Anything unusual?

Anything unusual. A zing in Jess's brain. Something that came to her attention in just those few minutes in the linen closet, something that caught her eye and then slipped away even before she stood up to leave. She closed her eyes, re-creating the scene in her mind, and tried to imagine those few moments. Exactly what did she see? What had caught her eye in an instant and faded just as quickly? Not her size. Not her long braids, and not her voice, which had been mannish for a small woman.

But something about her feet. That was it. Rosemary's feet.

The *whoop* sounded on Jess's phone first and then on Teddy's.

"Mom," Teddy said.

She checked the text.

Baby Ruby has disappeared.

"What does she say?" Jess asked.

"Same thing she says on yours. I knew that's exactly what she'd say," Teddy said.

"Me too."

Teddy could see Delilah with her torn dress, flying around the bedroom as if sheer movement had the capacity to make things better.

As if by rushing around the perimeter of the hotel room, deep breathing and talking too much, Baby Ruby might materialize.

"I don't want to see any of them," Jess said.

"Of course you don't."

They were quiet, side by side on the steps, their legs touching, pressing knee to knee.

"What are you going to say?" Jess asked quietly.

"What are *you* going to say?"

"Nothing," Jess said.

"You have to say something."

"First I have to think."

"I'm always the one in trouble but this time what has happened is not my trouble."

"I know."

"This time it's your trouble."

"I know that, Teddy, and I know you're just helping me out, and I know this is completely my fault and that my life is over and over and over unless I find her."

There was another *whoop* on both phones.

The staff tells me that Baby Ruby was KIDNAPPED and they've called the police and the police are here.

"So now what?" Teddy asked, taking out a cigarette.

"Now" — Jess threw her arm around Teddy's shoulder — "we have to divide and conquer. You do one thing and I do another and one of us will find her."

"So what are you going to do?" Teddy asked.

"I'm going to find the woman in the linen closet."

"How can you do that?"

"Because I have to find her and I think she *must* be in the hotel."

"And I'll go up to the room and deal with Mom and Dad and Whee and Danny and Beet and the police. Right?"

"Right."

"That's kind of a cop-out, Jess."

"If I go up there, they'll scream at me and say terrible things and nothing good will happen. If *you* go, you're not the one responsible for what happened. You will actually be able to help them. And maybe the police will find her."

Teddy rested her chin on her fists. Jess was right. Nothing good would happen anyway, but at least there was a better chance of finding Ruby if Teddy was with Delilah and Aldie and Danny and Beet, and all of them together could help the police.

"I hope you don't do anything stupid or dangerous," Teddy said.

"I won't."

"Or run away."

Jess was an optimist by nature. Mostly, she believed things would work out. But tonight she could not stop the moving picture that floated across her brain.

Baby Ruby gone for good. Days would pass without her. Weeks. Baby Ruby in the hospital. Or even worse.

"You have to promise you'll text," Teddy said. "Anything could happen. These guys are criminals."

"If I'm in trouble, I will text," Jess said. "And I'll always answer the phone if you call me."

Teddy texted Delilah.

Coming.

"Stay in touch," Teddy said, winding her arms around her sister's shoulders. "Be soooo careful."

~

Since her parents' divorce and the arrival of Delilah's boyfriends, since Teddy's departure for the Home for Girls with Problems, Jess had spent a lot of time alone. She had friends and parties and ice-skating and lacrosse camp in the summer, but after school, after sports and piano lessons, she came home to an empty house. Usually, she walked the dog first, and then, with trepidation, she checked the fridge to see what note Delilah had left for her. If she was going to be home to cook dinner, she didn't leave a note. But if she planned to be out, there was a cheery letter scrawled on lined paper:

"Dinner in the slow cooker, angel-puss. See you about ten. I'm on my cell so call if you need me."

Or best of all, sometimes there was a surprise note with good news:

"See you at six, angel-puss, and let's go get pizza. Finish your homework and maybe we can go to Sprinkles for a fudge sundae."

Angel-puss and ice cream! Angel-puss was her baby name, and ice cream — Jess hadn't eaten ice cream since a little donut roll of flesh had accumulated on her hips.

Nevertheless.

Every day it was the same. Jess would pick up the key under the flowerpot, let herself in the front door, walk the dog, get a banana out of the fruit bowl, call one of her friends just to blah blah blah for a while, do her homework, which was easy, and then she'd sit at the kitchen table, making up the kinds of stories she used to imagine when she and Teddy played SLEUTH.

Some nights, before her mother came home, she'd go up to her bedroom, the one she used to share with Teddy, and think about Teddy and how happy she had been when they played SLEUTH together after school. How she wished her sister were still in their house instead of the Home for Girls with Problems. How she wished Teddy had never started to shoplift so they could have had an ordinary life together as sisters and best friends.

When Teddy stepped out of the elevator on the sixth floor, she heard Delilah's voice flying down the corridor as if her voice had tiny feet. Teddy could hear every word she said from two corridors away.

"When is the last time anyone saw Baby Ruby?"

Two policemen were standing by the door and a third one, Detective Van Slyde, was taking notes.

"Where is Jess?" Delilah asked Teddy. "Do you know *anything*?"

From the bathroom, a high-pitched wail — a single unbroken note, a long straight line of sound.

Beet, Teddy thought, shivers down her spine. Teddy was not a calm girl, but she needed to be calm now.

"Teddy." Delilah's voice was hoarse and cracking. "Officer Van Slyde is the detective in charge of finding Baby Ruby and he wants to know, where is Jess?"

Teddy sat down beside her mother, a little breathless. The panic attacks she had been having, like the one at Whee's rehearsal dinner, came out of nowhere. Out of the blue, no known cause.

But this was a real emergency, and in a real emergency, she couldn't have a panic attack. An act of will. A decision.

"Have you seen her?" Delilah asked again, leaning on Teddy's shoulder.

"I have," Teddy said. "Baby Ruby disappeared from the room while Jess was in the bathroom. Jess is on her own search."

"What was she doing in the bathroom?"

"The bathroom door was closed."

"That's not what I asked. I asked why she was in the bathroom with the door closed and why, when you discovered that Ruby was gone, you didn't go immediately to the police or tell us. Come into the rehearsal dinner and tell me that she had been kidnapped."

Teddy hesitated, taking a deep breath.

"We just didn't. I came upstairs when I told you I was going to come upstairs."

"But you came back into the Bay Room as if nothing had happened *after* you knew."

"Teddy," Detective Van Slyde said. "This is a serious situation and we must have the truth as you know it. Where is your sister?"

"She has a clue. Not a big one. She's following a hunch."

"Where did you last see her?"

"In the lobby. I just came upstairs on the elevator and I could see her in the lobby leaning against a red leather couch as the doors closed. That was less than five minutes ago."

"They're locking down the hotel any minute, and with any luck, she is still in the hotel and she won't be able to get out," Detective Van Slyde said. "I'm going to radio a description of her."

"She's small," Teddy said. "A round face with freckles and slightly curly hair and bright blue eyes. A little plump. Just a little."

Detective Van Slyde called in the description.

"Wearing?" he asked.

"Pink shirt, jeans, and sneakers."

"Send out an alert and track her down," he said to the officer on the phone. "So what happened when you came upstairs from the rehearsal dinner?"

"I got a text from my sister more or less saying there was an emergency and I rushed up here to the room."

"And your sister was here?"

"No, she wasn't here. Whee, my about-to-be-married sister, has a wedding dress that had been hanging in the bathroom. When I got here, there was a cleaning lady and the dress had been thrown across the bed. In the bathroom, Whee's new makeup was all over the place."

Beet was coming out of the bathroom, little hiccups of tears. She sat down with Danny on the side of the bed, holding his hand.

"Whee doesn't know yet," Delilah said. "She and Victor are out with their friends. She's going to die."

"My life is ruined," Beet said, trying to catch her breath.

Teddy sat down on the bed beside Beet and put her arm around her.

"I am so afraid," Beet said, resting her head on Teddy's shoulder.

Detective Van Slyde had pulled up a chair and was taking notes.

"My sister was babysitting," Danny said. "They were in this room and the door was locked and there was nothing Jess needed to do except give Ruby a bottle of milk — I'd left it all fixed for the baby. How could this have happened?"

"Where is the babysitter now?"

"My sister, my little sister, Jess," Danny was saying. "I don't know. They are both gone, right, Teddy?"

"Baby Ruby is gone," Teddy said quietly.

She gave the detective information about herself, that she was the third child in the O'Fines family, that she should be in high school but was not. Instead, she was living at the Home for Girls with Problems, news that seemed only slightly interesting to the detective. He made no comment.

"If you think I had anything to do with this," Teddy said. "I did not. But I read mysteries and I know a lot about crime and I know that often it's someone in the family who is to blame."

"I'm just collecting factual information about your sister's circumstances, you understand."

"I do," Teddy said. "When Whee and I left to go downstairs for the rehearsal dinner, Jess watched us — watched me and Whee walk to the elevators. And waiting for the elevator with us was a small man in a green shirt." She took a deep breath, her heart sounding in her ears. "But when the elevator came, he didn't get on. Instead, he headed toward Jess and Baby Ruby. Jess thought he was a little creepy, so she backed into the room and shut the door or *thinks she shut the door*. And then she put Ruby down on a towel on the floor on her back like you told her to do, Danny, and then she went into the bathroom and shut the door."

"Why in the world did she shut the door?" Danny asked. "She was supposed to be BABYsitting."

"Teddy?" Delilah was wringing her hands.

"What did Jess tell you she was doing in the bathroom?"

Teddy didn't reply.

She was not going to say that Jess had been putting on Whee's makeup or that she had tried on Whee's precious wedding dress or that she had possibly, even probably, forgotten to shut the door completely when she went back in the room.

What she wanted to say was:

JESS HAS BEEN WAITING ALL YEAR TO COME TO WHEE'S
WEDDING AND SHE HAD A NEW DRESS AND AT THE LAST
MINUTE DANNY MADE HER BABYSIT BECAUSE HE WAS TOO
MUCH OF A LOSER TO GET A BABYSITTER ON HIS OWN.

But she didn't say anything. She sat quietly at the end of the bed
and tried to block out the sounds of her family's voices.

By nature, and since she could remember, Teddy had worried. She
worried that she would never get out of the Home for Girls with
Problems or that she would be released and go back to shoplifting, that
her parents didn't really love her because she had caused them so much
trouble. She worried that she was the real reason for their divorce, that
she'd never have an ordinary life, that she'd end up in a hospital with
panic attacks and the doctors would give her the wrong medicine and
the medicine would kill her. That kind of worry.

Which is how she saw her world.

Full of sadness that would never get better and problems that
would never be solved.

Not like cheery Jess O'Fines, who believed if there was a problem,
she could be the one to fix it.

As far as Teddy knew, the only thing that she had ever been able to
do very well was to shoplift. And that, as Delilah told her, didn't count
as an accomplishment.

Detective Van Slyde raised his hand and asked for quiet.

"We have a lockdown on the hotel as of now. Kidnapping or suspected kidnapping is taken very seriously. We will be interviewing members of the staff, guests at the hotel, and all of you. We need every bit of information we can get."

"Where will you be?" Delilah asked.

"I'll be here," Detective Van Slyde said. "I am not leaving this hotel tonight."

Delilah sat down next to Teddy, very close, too close, speaking to her in a whisper.

"I know you have some clue about what happened and you just aren't speaking."

Teddy shook her head.

"At least you know what Jess was doing instead of watching the baby. You know that, right?"

"Talk, Teddy. Say something," Beet said. "You're making it worse."

"I have nothing to say," Teddy said.

She heard the *whoop* in her chest where she had stuck her cell phone under the straps of her bra.

Detective Van Slyde leaned forward and touched Teddy's arm.

"Did you see the man your sister mentioned?"

"Twice, but the first time, I don't remember what he looked like, only what Jess told me," Teddy said. "He was standing by the elevators when I got on the elevator with Whee to go to the dinner and then, according to Jess, he headed in the direction of our room where Jess was standing with the baby."

"That was the first time?"

"Yes. And the second time was after Baby Ruby disappeared. Just a little while ago, he bolted. Jess was following him from the elevator into the lower level parking lot and he ran fast and then tore around the parking lot in his car. I was with her."

"Can you describe him?" Van Slyde asked.

"He's wearing a green shirt the color of pistachio ice cream," Teddy said. "And he's small. Very small."

"Hair color? Trousers? Shoes?"

"His hair is dark and straight. I didn't notice the shoes and pants."

"And do you know where your sister is?"

Teddy hesitated.

"I left her downstairs in the lobby," Teddy said. "She was going to look for Ruby on her own but that was a while ago."

"Risky," Detective Van Slyde said. "How long ago?"

"Ten minutes, fifteen, maybe."

"Before the lockdown." He noted it in his book.

While Detective Van Slyde wrote in his notebook, Teddy turned away and, hiding the phone, checked her message.

Headed out of the hotel. ON FOOT. I'll stay in touch.

Jess walked back through the revolving doors into the lobby. The parties were breaking up, lines by the elevators, partygoers on their way back to their rooms. The music had stopped playing, and the lights were dim. Her plan was to go up to the linen closet on the sixth floor, look around, ask the housekeeping staff, if any of them were still awake, if they know this lady, Rosemary, small with tiny feet, a rosemary smell, and loopy braids. Maybe if Jess was casual enough not to alarm them by seeming too interested, one of the staff would give her some information. After all, if Rosemary *was* in the linen closet, someone else besides Jess should have seen her. And if she was in a room where domestic staff came in and out, they must know something about her.

At least that is how Jess was thinking when she walked across the lobby on her way to the bank of elevators and saw someone who took her breath away.

A woman with loopy braids framing her face. She had on a flowered skirt, full, which hung to her ankles, and a white billowy blouse — not what Rosemary had been wearing when Jess saw her in the linen closet, but it was Rosemary. She was wearing flip-flops, too large for her tiny feet, which slapped the marble floor as she walked across the lobby in front of the registration desk. She passed the concierge's desk and a group of young stragglers from the dance, heading toward the revolving doors at the front of the hotel where taxis lined up.

Jess had a sudden intake of breath, a cramp in her stomach. Breathless, she followed the woman as she moved through the lobby on tiny feet so swift that Jess had trouble keeping up without running. Through the door she went, past the doorman, and when Jess came out of the hotel, Rosemary was gone.

The woman must have slipped in front of the doorman, traveling like a crab, scuttling in her flip-flops. Just as Jess passed him — holding the door open for a family in front of her — Rosemary disappeared.

Jess stopped and looked around. The family was getting in a cab. A young man was standing with a girl, maybe his girlfriend, his hand on the small of her back, her chin upturned. He was kissing her, which arrested Jess's attention for the shortest time but long enough that when she looked beyond the couple, past the taxi cabs parked along the curb waiting for passengers, she saw no one who met the description of Rosemary.

Jess leaned against a pillar. She took her phone out of her pocket and texted Teddy.

Headed out of the hotel. ON FOOT. I'll stay in touch.

Jess wasn't sure what she was looking for, but she walked along the line of cabs and beyond, down the hill, toward the water, cars parked along the curb, mostly empty. Somewhere in the darkness, Rosemary had evaporated.

A young man, very young, maybe under driving age, was sitting in the front seat of an open jeep, the engine running, music playing on the radio. Jess walked past the jeep, glancing at the man without turning her head, past the next car with its blinkers on, the front seat reclined, the driver shining in the streetlight, his eyes closed. Another car, but it was empty, and then a small car with a man or maybe a woman wearing a baseball cap seated in the driver's seat, hands on the wheel, the engine on. Someone, a shadow of someone, was in the back, maybe a child, her head just skimming the top of the seat.

Jess wasn't even thinking as she walked past, her arms swinging. Her jeans too tight, caught between her legs and uncomfortable. She stopped to tug on them, and as she did, an arm shot out from the open window of the driver's side of the car and grabbed her.

It happened quickly. Her arm pulled against the car, an open door, the sound of grunting. She was dragged across the lap of the man who had hold of her, the steering wheel burrowing into her back. Then something was tied around her eyes so she couldn't see, her hands tied behind her back, and though she was struggling, kicking hard enough to stop a man, she couldn't stop *this* man.

And then she was on the floor of the front seat of the car, the car moving, music playing very loud, but not as loud in her ears as the beating of her heart.

CHAPTER TEN

ROOM 618

When Whee arrived, smiling for the first time in days, Beet had locked herself in the bathroom.

Danny was lying facedown across the bed, and in room 618, the rest of the O'Fines family paced. They had been told by Detective Van Slyde to *Stay put* and he would be in touch. Police all over the city were on the lookout, he told them.

In the locked-down hotel, police were interviewing the guests and staff.

"*Stay put* is not going to be possible for me," Delilah said. "If we don't hear from the police in half an hour, I'm going downstairs."

Teddy lay on her back, her feet on the bed, and looked at the ceiling. She was breathing through her mouth. The therapist at the Home had taught her deep breathing to avoid a full-on panic attack — drag the air through the mouth, down, down into the stomach, she advised.

She ought to be able to help with a stolen baby, she was thinking.

After all, she was an expert at stealing. A professional. She knew what it felt like to *need* to take something. But could you *need* to take a baby? Was it that specific? Could anything else be satisfying to steal? Like jewelry or a dress or a puppy? Even a puppy?

Or maybe they wanted to *sell* the baby. They needed money. How much would a baby sell for and who would buy one? She was asking herself these questions, the same kinds of question she and Jess used to ask solving crimes when they were playing SLEUTH, when Whee walked in the room.

Whee was giggling, actually giggling, the way she used to do before she decided to marry Victor Treat.

"You tell Whee, Teddy," Delilah said in a stage whisper. "I can't."

"Please," Aldie added. "Whee is going to collapse if we have to call off the wedding."

Teddy, the kleptomaniac, the incarcerated troubled O'Fines daughter, was becoming the adult in room 618, the one holding it all together.

But Whee recognized trouble before Teddy had a chance to speak.

"What is going on?" she asked.

"Ruby's gone," Danny said.

"Gone?"

"Gone. Stolen."

"Kidnapped," Aldie said. "While we were at the rehearsal dinner, someone came in the room and took her."

"Someone?"

"Jess was in the bathroom with the door shut," Delilah said.

Whee sank down on the end of the bed, moving Danny's feet out of the way.

"Where is Jess now?"

"Gone," Delilah said.

"Jess is gone?"

"We don't know where Jess is. She is simply not here," Delilah said. "And she doesn't answer her phone."

"She's looking for Ruby," Teddy said, sitting down next to Whee,

"What was she doing in the bathroom with the door shut?" Whee asked.

"That's my question." Danny had scooted to the end of the bed and was sitting next to Whee. "She was supposed to be babysitting, so what was she doing in the bathroom long enough for Baby Ruby to disappear?"

Whee got up from the bed and turned the knob on the bathroom door.

"Locked," she said.

"Beet is in there," Danny said.

"No wonder, poor thing." Whee knocked. "Beet? Can I come in?"

Moments passed and the door clicked and opened, and Beet walked out, crossed the room to the long window overlooking the ocean, and banged on it with her fists.

The bathroom was dark. Whee turned on the light and walked in. Teddy could see her unzipping the protective bag in which her wedding dress was hanging.

"Teddy?" she called.

Teddy slipped in the door, closing it behind her.

"The police think she'll be found, don't they?"

"They hope so," Teddy said. "Jess wasn't in the bathroom very long. When she came out and saw that Ruby was gone and she texted me and we both . . ." She didn't finish.

Maybe half an hour had passed, maybe more before the police were notified by the staff at the hotel, and by then news had gotten out from the cleaning staff on the sixth floor that a baby had disappeared. Even guests at the hotel had overheard the conversation about Ruby and passed it on to others.

Whee took the dress out of the bag, holding it away from her body, looking at it, examining the bodice, bringing it under the light over the sink.

When she looked up, her eyes were full of tears.

"It's too much emotion for me. Baby Ruby and then Jess. And just minutes ago, I was getting married and now I'm not getting married."

"Lipstick?" Teddy asked, looking at the dress.

Whee nodded.

"The dress doesn't matter. Only Ruby matters — but Jess should never have been left in charge."

"Jess is perfectly capable of being in charge," Teddy said quietly. "Of anything. She just shouldn't have been *made* to babysit."

Her phone rang its cheerful jangly song and she picked it up.

"This is Detective Van Slyde," he said. "I'm checking to see if you have seen your sister?"

"I haven't," Teddy said, a sinking feeling in her blood.

"Have you heard from her?"

"I haven't heard anything. I called but there was no answer." She caught her breath. "Why?"

"Just information that we need," he said. "If you can reach her, let me know right away."

"I'll text her," Teddy said.

Teddy hung up and texted Jess.

What's up. You okay?

She waited. Nothing. Minutes passed. Ten. Fifteen. Nothing.

She would not tell her parents. There was already too much bad news.

Jess lay with her cheek resting against the rough carpet on the floor of the car. She should be frightened and she was — the blood was rushing through her veins, her heart was racing. But she was also strangely calm. She didn't struggle against the ties on her wrists or legs. She felt her body sink into the carpet.

But her ears were acutely tuned. She listened for every rustle, every turn of the automobile, every breath that she could hear above the radio.

The car smelled of something she knew, beer maybe, the tangy, slightly moldy smell of her father's beer, and something else.

They were making a lot of turns, first right, then left, then right again, a short drive, and right a third time. Then suddenly the radio was turned off and the car was eerily silent.

No sound at all but the hush of breath.

It was as if she were trapped in a cave and something she could not see was about to happen.

And then the accumulating smell of rosemary. The smell gathered, moving over the backseat to the front and sinking to the floor, where Jess was lying facedown, her head turned just slightly, but sufficient for the smell to permeate the air around her.

Even then, it didn't occur to Jess to be afraid, to think that something was going to happen to her. Her only thought was Baby Ruby and a clear hunch that she was about to find out where she was.

"You were late to pick me up at the hotel." It was a woman's voice from the backseat. "What are we doing now?"

"We're going to the flats," the man said.

"I don't want to go to the flats, baby," she said.

"We have to."

"I want to go to the cemetery first."

"No, Angel. It's dark, dark and the middle of the night. We are not going to the cemetery."

There was soft crying from the backseat.

"I'm not ready to leave Los Angeles without going to the cemetery first."

She had an accent. The man did not. Her English was clear, easy for Jess to understand, the *i* pronounced like a long *e*, each syllable articulated. *Maybe French or Italian or Spanish*, Jess thought. Probably Spanish if she was the same woman Jess had seen in the linen closet.

"We'll go to the flats, pick up what we need, and get out at dawn, before the sun comes up."

"To where? You said we will go to Canada."

"We'll take the first plane out to wherever it's going."

"And then to Canada."

"We need a passport."

"I have a passport."

"I don't, Angel. We'll find a way. We'd be better to fly to somewhere in America. Like Omaha or Toledo or Indianapolis, someplace unexpected and not too far, and then get a car and find a small town."

"I want to go to Canada."

"I know you want to go to Canada."

"And first, before the flats, I have to go to the cemetery."

"If you insist," the man said, resigned.

"What about the girl?" she piped up again.

"The girl was a surprise. She walked by the car, that's all. She walked by and I thought —" He stopped short.

"Are you turning in here?"

There was silence.

"Are you? Are you turning, Jack?"

"I am. I said I would and I am."

Jess felt the turn to the left because it was sharp, a squeaking of brakes, and then the car slowed over gravel and stopped.

They opened the doors.

"Are you sure we're allowed to be here at night, Angel?"

"Why not? They would lock the gates if we were not allowed, and they didn't."

The man grunted.

Jack, Jess thought. She wondered if she had seen him before, if he was the small man she thought he was, and he had pulled her into the car because he recognized her. He had seen her before, standing with Ruby outside room 618. He had seen her chase him into the garage.

"The kids from the high school have sex here because it's dark."

"So they leave the place open for the kids to have sex? I don't think so, Angel."

The doors shut.

They seemed to be gone a very long time. Jess couldn't tell. Her cell phone vibrated in the pocket of her jeans but her hands were tied. Certainly it was Teddy. She had told Teddy she was leaving the hotel. Someone might have seen her leave, maybe even seen her pulled into the car. But if that were true, they would have followed the car and they would have found her by now.

It must be the cemetery where the car was parked — gates, kids having sex, that sort of thing.

Jess knew a lot about sex mainly from Teddy and she was interested. But sex in a cemetery?

What was *in* the cemetery? Who had died? Was it a child in the cemetery?

Of course not *Baby Ruby*, Jess thought, trying to be very reasonable, although she imagined the worst. Too short a time had passed. Four hours at the most.

Baby Ruby was a screamer. That worried Jess. A screamer was hard to kidnap. Too much noise. Whoever had taken her from the room would want her to *stop* screaming.

They were back in the car, the woman weeping again.

"Now to the flats."

"Is it safe?" the woman asked.

"Safe?"

"Safe for us to go there and do what we have to do."

"Nothing's safe, darling. We made this decision together. Remember?"

"I remember."

He turned the radio on again to Jess's relief. She was listening to a conversation she didn't understand and it made her nervous. She knew that what she didn't know must have to do with Baby Ruby. Otherwise, Jess would be no use to these people. No reason to tie her hands and legs, to put her in the bottom of their stinky car.

"What about the girl?" the woman, Angel, asked again.

"The girl?" Jack said. "We'll get to that problem when we arrive at the flats."

"What are you thinking of, Jack?"

"Nothing. I'm thinking of nothing. I wasn't expecting the girl and there she was and stupidly I dragged her into the car. *Now what?* That's what I'm thinking."

CHAPTER ELEVEN

TOO MUCH TIME TO THINK

The police were not ruling out that a guest at the hotel had kidnapped Ruby. In fact, that was the most likely scenario in kidnappings, Detective Van Slyde told them. One of the risks of hotels is that they don't check out the backgrounds of the guests. Anyone who has a credit card in good standing can make a reservation.

"We're on this case," the detective said. "And I know how hard it is to wait for more information to come in."

"I can't wait," Delilah said. "It's not in my temperament. If something's the matter, I need a task."

"I'm afraid your job is to wait, Mrs. O'Fines."

Danny was weeping.

"I feel like you think this is my fault," he said. "All of you except Mom."

"It's not your fault, Danny," Beet said. "All you did was blow the babysitter job."

Teddy sat down beside him on the end of the bed.

"It's just an awful thing that happened," she said.

Growing up, Teddy had not liked Danny. He was selfish and self-centered and called her stupid. *You're okay, Ted,* he'd say. *Just a little stupid.*

But since he'd married Beet, she thought of him as a *wimp.*

Now she put her arm around him, rested her head on his shoulder, and consoled him.

"Jess will find Ruby," she said. "She's very brave and she has instincts."

"I told her not to take her eyes off Ruby the whole night."

"Shut up, Danny," Beet said from the corner of the room where she sat curled in a ball with her head down.

"She has the instincts to figure things out," Teddy said. "I bet right this minute she has a hunch about Baby Ruby and she's following her instincts."

"So why doesn't she answer the phone?"

"She's too busy," Teddy said.

"Finding Ruby?" Danny asked quietly.

"Finding Ruby."

———

Detective Van Slyde, on his cell phone, had moved to the door to leave, but he motioned Teddy to come over.

"I don't have much to tell you but we're working on this."

"What about Jess?" Teddy asked.

He shook his head. "Why didn't she let us know when this happened?"

"She was embarrassed, I guess. Or ashamed. She's a really responsible girl," Teddy said. "I wouldn't want you to get the wrong impression."

"I don't have the wrong impression. You'll let me know if you hear anything at all. I'm going back down to the security office if you need me."

He shut the door.

"I never trusted the police," Aldie was saying. "I grew up at a moment in time when trusting the police was a mistake."

"What moment in time was that, Aldie?" Delilah asked.

"Same moment that you grew up," Aldie said.

"Don't argue," Beet said. "Please don't argue."

Teddy leaned against the wall next to the door and took out her cell.

Where are you? she texted. **ARE YOU OKAY?**

Still there was no response.

Jess was not okay or else she would text back. She would say *help* if she needed help. If it were possible, she would alert Teddy to trouble.

"Listen, you guys. I think we should go downstairs and sit in the lobby," Teddy said, addressing her family scattered around the room. "It's too intense locked in this room together."

"I'm not going anyplace," Danny said.

"Me neither," Delilah said. "We can't be in public, Teddy. We're too upset."

"Then if we're going to be here stuffed in this room," Teddy said, "we have to be a family."

"We are a family already," Delilah said.

"Then we have to be a good one."

"However terrible we feel, we have to pull together," Delilah said.

No one spoke. Whee was arranging the pearls on the bodice of her dress to conceal the mark of lipstick. Beet was in the corner, her knees up, her head resting on her arms. Danny sat in a chair in front of the television screen, his head thrown back, his hands locked in a tight fist. And Aldie paced.

Delilah had taken a notebook out of her bag and was furiously writing.

"Notes to help the police," she said to no one in particular. "I can't just sit around and wait. I don't have the temperament for it."

Teddy *was* the one holding her family together. Teddy O'Fines, juvenile delinquent, high school dropout, kleptomaniac, the humiliation of her parents, the child least likely to succeed, was the one in charge.

She sat down beside Beet. Sat there without speaking, close but not too close, absorbing the heat of Beet's anguish just being beside her.

She had risen to the occasion of her family's disaster and somehow, looking around the room at each of them, she was beginning to feel affection for Delilah and Beet, even for Danny, surprising affection that she had not felt since her parents divorced.

The road to the flats was bumpy. Jess tried to keep her head off the floor by straining her neck so that she didn't bump it over and over as they drove the rough terrain. If they left her in the car while they packed to go to Omaha or Canada or wherever it was they planned to go, if they left her for long enough so that she could untie the cords holding her wrists together, or wrest out the stuffing they had pushed into her mouth to keep her from making too much noise, then she could escape to text Teddy for help.

The car stopped. Someone opened a window and Jess felt a breeze brush over her back, heard the sound of rain.

"Jack, do you see that Bono is standing right in front of us under the hood of his truck?" Angel said from the backseat.

"I see him."

"So he'll know we're getting out of town and he'll tell. He could even tell the police. You know Bono. He'll tell on anyone for a dollar."

"He won't know anything if we're careful. Just go in the building, pack up — we don't need much — slip outside when he's not looking."

"We've got to speak to Bono or he'll be suspicious."

"So speak to him. Say hey, Bono, just getting a couple of things my sister left at the flats."

"What about the girl?" Angel asked.

"I'm covering her with a blanket so no one can see I've got a girl in the car," he said. "This won't take five minutes and then we're out of here, on the way to your sister's and freedom."

The door opened — something heavy was dropped on Jess and the door shut.

"Hey, Bono," Jack said. "How's it going?"

Jess couldn't hear the response from the man, Bono, but she did hear Jack's muffled voice say, "Not true, Bono. Just more bad talk from the flats."

And then the voices were gone. Jess assumed that Jack and Angel had gone into the flats, whatever the flats were, and that the man Bono was still working on his truck, and it frightened her to think that someone could peer into the car and make out the shape of a girl under a blanket and *do* something to her.

She needed a plan. So far she was piecing together a part of the story — where she was, what Angel and Jack were doing. She imagined the flats were a dangerous part of Los Angeles where desperate people lived who had guns and didn't care what they did to hurt other people. Even Angel seemed to be afraid of the flats, although it appeared she lived there. She had things to pick up necessary for their trip to Omaha or Indianapolis.

Whether or not Angel and Jack had anything to do with Ruby, Jess guessed they were escaping Los Angeles because they had done something bad, something illegal, or they had committed a crime and the police were looking for them.

If they *were* the ones who had stolen Baby Ruby, then perhaps they were taking Ruby on their escape. Or possibly Baby Ruby was at the sister's house. Or maybe Jack and Angel were *not* the ones who had kidnapped Baby Ruby and were in trouble for other reasons.

But if that were true, why would Jack have run away from Jess in the parking garage or pulled her into the car and tied her up? And why would Angel — it must have been Angel smelling of rosemary in the linen closet — have been hiding?

As long as Jess was tied up on the floor of the front seat of the stinky car and not dumped on some road or in some building like the flats, as long as she was alive, then there was still a chance that she would find Baby Ruby, or Ruby would reappear somewhere, at the sister's or in the flats or at the airport.

And if nothing happened to Jess, then there was a chance Baby Ruby would materialize and Jess could grab her and run.

That was her thinking when Angel and Jack opened the car doors and climbed in. They didn't talk. Jack turned on the engine and drove out slowly. Angel was crying, little half sobs coming from the backseat.

"Not so bad," Jack said.

"I think Bono's going to call the police."

"He doesn't have a phone, Angel. He'd have to get his car working again and drive to the station."

"That could happen."

"Unlikely," Jack said.

And then they were silent.

Jess was beginning to feel sick, stuck in the front seat with no room and no fresh air to breathe and the awful smell of the carpet on the floor of the car. Then the car turned left, then right, then right again, one street after the other.

"I'm getting carsick," Angel said.

"Get a grip, Angel. We're almost at your sister's and she's got bus tickets."

"Bus tickets? You said we were taking an airplane and we're not even going to Canada."

"We're taking a bus to Oregon and then we're flying somewhere but not to Canada. I told you that."

"You told me we weren't going to Canada. Not about the bus."

"Your sister didn't think it was a good idea to go to the airport where there are all those inspections to make sure you're not carrying a bomb. So she got bus tickets for us."

Angel was crying again and then she stopped and they were driving for what seemed a very long time and then the car stopped.

"So here we are," Jack said.

"Jack?"

"No more problems, please, Angel."

"I don't want to leave Elena here."

"We're too far down the road to turn back. You were the one who wanted do this. Not me. I went along because I love you and now you are driving me crazy."

"But what about Elena?"

"Elena is dead, Angel. We have to get out of the car now, go into your sister's, and do what we planned to do."

"What about the girl?"

"We're leaving the girl."

"In the car?"

"Here, at your sister's, in the car, and your sister can drive us to the bus station."

"We can't do that. The girl's heard us talking. She knows our names."

"Listen, Angel. Who's to say anyone is going to find her?"

"They'll find her if you're planning to just leave a car with a girl tied up in it. She'll say our names. And the police will know who we are. They'll be waiting for us at the bus station in Oregon."

A car door opened and Jess heard a woman's voice.

"Come on in," the woman said. "There's a bus goes early tomorrow. Six a.m. You can spend the night here."

"I think we should get out tonight," Angel said. "The police are clued in."

"Then you're going to have to drive," the woman said. "No buses until tomorrow morning."

"But we've got a girl on the floor of the front seat."

"What girl?" the woman asked.

The car doors closed then and Jess was alone again.

So that was the sister, Jess thought. They were at the sister's house.

And what about this girl Elena? Dead Elena. Was she the one in the cemetery?

She tried to turn over but could not. There wasn't enough room in the bottom of the car to move at all. She rubbed her wrists together, hoping to loosen the rope tying them, but they were bound too tight.

The phone in her back pocket rang and rang. Then a *whoop*. Likely Teddy.

If she was quiet and careful not to move, if she let herself sink into the stinky carpet, then she might fall asleep. Struggling to free herself wouldn't make a difference. The ties were tight and she was trapped in too small a place. A strange sleepiness was overtaking her and she was surprised at how calm she felt. Better to sleep. With no hope of escaping, she had too much time to think.

CHAPTER TWELVE

TOO LATE?

Teddy was scrunched between the bed and Whee's giant suitcase, her head in her hands, staring at a stain on the carpet, her heart beating as if it had jumped into her mouth. Delilah didn't help. Teddy could see her leaning against the closet door, her eyes closed. From time to time, a plaintive animal sound escaped from deep inside her, and then Danny's loud voice:

"PLEASE, Mom."

"Teddy?"

It was Delilah.

"Do *something*," she said. "So far no one is doing anything useful."

"What can I do, Mom?" Teddy asked. She was thinking the worst, as she tended to do.

Maybe it was already too late, not just for Baby Ruby but also for Jess.

She had called Jess at least fifteen times — *whoop, whoop, whoop,* and on and on. And there was no answer. Teddy was certain Jess was somewhere she should not be.

"Teddy?" Delilah asked. "Maybe if you went to Detective Van Slyde by yourself. Maybe he'd give you some information. The police have to have some information by now."

"I'll do that, Mom," Teddy said, heading toward the door just as Victor Treat was arriving.

"So, guys," Victor said, addressing the room. "What we need to do is cancel the wedding."

"Cancel the wedding?" Delilah said. "The wedding is planned. It's set to go. We will have the wedding tomorrow afternoon at the Brambles Hotel."

"Don't be a martyr," Beet said from her corner of the room. "Of course you'll have the wedding whether we're there or not."

"Let's wait," Aldie said. "I'm optimistic. I'm very optimistic."

"You don't stop the wedding just because —" Delilah began.

Whee got up, crossed the room, and went into the bathroom.

"Everyone is fighting because we're all on edge," she said and closed the door.

And quickly, before anything else got said, Teddy fled the room.

━━━

Things were bad enough with Baby Ruby missing, but now Jess. If Baby Ruby wasn't recovered by morning, Teddy imagined the O'Fines family exploding in little pieces all over the Brambles Hotel.

Teddy stepped into the elevator, her head down so she didn't have to look at herself in the mirror. She wasn't aware that someone was already in the elevator, going down in the middle of the night. She saw her in the mirror — the same woman with whom she had ridden earlier that evening.

"Oh, hello," the woman said. "So nice to see you."

Teddy folded her arms across her chest, avoiding eye contract.

"I was at my niece Miranda duFall's wedding, my great-niece. Do you know her?"

"No," Teddy said. "I don't."

"Well, it was just lovely," she said, looking in the mirror, pushing hairpins into her chignon. "I like a good wedding, don't you? And then it was over and I went up to the twelfth floor, but my room isn't on the twelfth floor, and now I simply can't remember for the life of me where my room is."

There was a pause.

"Do you happen to know where my room might be?" she asked.

"I don't," Teddy said.

"And this hoopla. Do you know about the hoopla?"

Teddy shook her head.

"Well, a baby has been kidnapped. A little baby girl from the sixth floor. That's what I heard."

The elevator stopped at three and Teddy got off. She walked the rest of the way downstairs and went across the lobby to the office where Detective Van Slyde should be, and there he was on the telephone.

"News?" he said, still on the phone.

She pulled up a chair beside him.

"I can't reach Jess," she said. "I keep trying."

"We are doing everything we can. They're searching for her everywhere, a full-court press."

"What do you think?"

"We don't think anything yet, but we're investigating everything and interviewing everyone and trying to keep the gossip level down while we talk to people."

"I don't understand."

"Our job is information. We follow every lead until it proves to be a dead end. Time is important. We know what time your baby disappeared from your room, and anything could have happened. We need to work fast."

"So what you're thinking . . ."

"Someone took Ruby and that someone had to be either on the staff or a guest in the hotel."

"Jess saw a woman in the linen closet on the sixth floor. She was just sitting on the floor where all the sheets and towels are kept."

"What was Jess doing in the linen closet?"

"Hiding."

"And the woman?"

"That's all I know."

Jess rubbed her wrists together, back and forth, back and forth, back and forth, hoping to loosen the ties. She began to feel a little give, as if it might be possible to stretch them slightly, enough to wriggle her left hand, her smaller hand, out of the grip of the rope.

Her shoulders were tense. So was her back and stomach. Her head felt detached from her body, like a heavy wooden box sitting on her shoulders. If Jess didn't find Ruby, she would *die*. If she didn't actually die of shame and sadness, she would go to a poor country and work in an orphanage until she was very old.

She could see light, probably slipping under the cloth tied around her head covering her eyes, possibly from a streetlight.

Jack and Angel had been gone a long time. At least it felt as if they had been gone a long time. Every now and then, she stopped to listen. The windows of the car were shut, but she could hear a few cars driving by, though none stopped. She thought she heard the sound of shouting. She tried to be very still so she could hear what was being said but couldn't make out the words or whether they were coming from a man or a woman.

And then there was a fight.

Two women screaming at each other and Jess could hear them clearly. The voices were moving closer to the car.

"You helped me, yes, but you never asked for any money and I don't have it to give you!"

"You should have let me know that. I would have done nothing. Nothing if I had known you were going to do this to me!"

"Do what to you?"

"What you done. Ask me to help you out and then just scramble off with the goods and leave me poor as ever!"

"So what do you want?"

"A thousand dollars."

"What about the girl? I could give you the girl and you could ask for money to give her back. These families who go to the Brambles are rich."

"I don't want the girl."

"You don't want the girl?"

"That's what I said. I don't want the girl."

"What do you suggest?"

"Dump her in the ocean."

"You're a terrible woman, Maria. I wouldn't do that. She's a girl."

"So?"

And the door to the car opened. Someone was getting in the back-seat and the door closed.

Rosemary.

Jess could tell that it was Angel in the backseat and she was whimpering.

The door opened by the front seat, the key in the ignition, the engine on.

"What did you expect, Angel?" said Jack.

"We don't have a thousand dollars."

"You're right. We don't."

"Then we have to get it."

"How?"

"Use the girl. We can use the girl."

The car was moving slowly.

"Those people have money. They'll pay to get her back."

"This is too complicated for me, Angel. We're going to be in trouble and then we'll have nothing. Not each other, not a life. Nothing."

The car was going in circles, round and round, right turn after right turn, Angel whimpering in the backseat.

Jess lay very still.

"I'd rather get the money from the 7-Eleven than use the girl."

"Rob the 7-Eleven?"

"It's faster."

"You think a 7-Eleven has one thousand dollars in its cash register?"

"I don't know, Angel, darling. Maybe they only have five dollars. But it's night, they've been open all day. We drive by. See if the 7-Eleven is empty, and if it's empty, I go in, tie the guy up if there's only one guy. I won't go in if there's two."

"But you wouldn't know how to open the cash register."

"I've been around. I'd ask for a pack of cigarettes, give him a ten, he'd open the cash register, and then I'd jump the counter, tie him up, take what's in the drawer, and stroll out with my cigarettes."

"And what about the girl?"

"I don't know what about the girl. Maybe drive north and leave her on the beach. Let me find an empty 7-Eleven around here and see if I come out with one thousand dollars, and then we'll decide about the girl."

"We'll go back to Maria's first and give her the money."

"That's what we'll do, baby."

The car was quiet except for the sound of Angel whimpering. They were moving at a normal pace and Jess heard the *whoop* of a text message.

Angel heard it too.

"Did you hear that?"

"I did," he said.

"It's a cell phone."

"It is."

"The girl got a text message."

"I'm sure you're right, Angel."

"Get it from her and read it."

The car pulled to the right and stopped.

"Read the text to me and then throw the phone out the window."

Jess lay very still while he lifted the blanket, took the phone out of her back pocket, and replaced the blanket over her.

Her heart was beating too fast. If she lost her phone, then what?

JESS, it said. **Call me. We're terrified about you.**

And then Jess heard the sound of a window opening and the crack of the phone as it hit the pavement and the car was moving again.

The man turned on the radio to a music station, turned it up so the sound of Latin music filled the car.

"What did you do that for?" Angel called from the backseat.

"To relax, baby."

"It's making me feel worse."

"Listen, Angel. With any luck, I'm about to rob a 7-Eleven and come out with one thousand dollars to pay your sister, and I haven't got the nerve to do this if you are crying in the backseat. So I turned on the radio."

"Well, turn it off."

Nothing happened for a while except a tapping of his hand on the steering wheel and then he turned the music down but not off.

"Do you think someone will find the girl's phone?"

"Of course they'll find it."

"And then find out who it belongs to and then find us."

He had begun to sing along with the music in a low, melancholy voice. Jess, her cheek against the carpet, felt panic setting in. The smell of the carpet, the tightness of the ties around her wrists and ankles, a rising fear that Ruby was gone forever. If she saw her family again, they would not speak to her. Poor Danny. Ruby was his only joy. And Whee, her dress smudged with stolen makeup, her wedding ruined, and her mom — crazy Delilah. Jess would be sent to one of those places that people go when they are sick from a broken heart.

Only Teddy would forgive her, but too late.

Whoop, whoop sounded in Jess's head and she pretended it was Teddy texting.

What's going on? she imagined Teddy texting. **You could've ditched the country and headed to Kathmandu for all I know. I'm sitting up in bed**

in the middle of the night and it is almost morning and I haven't slept at all and NO WORD FROM YOU.

Whoop, whoop.

> Ted, I have been kidnapped by the kidnappers. Lying facedown in the front of this guy's car, tied up on the floor, and the carpet smells of pee and gasoline. I'll probably die in the next hour. I love you. Your favorite sister.

Whoop, whoop.

> Negative. You're not going to die. You're going to find this baby and bring her back to her parents and everyone will be so happy that they'll forget it ever happened because you are my amazing sister and you can do anything.

Sometime in the midst of pretending to text, the music playing, the car moving, but slowly, Jess fell asleep.

CHAPTER THIRTEEN

A TURN OF EVENTS

Teddy was sitting on the couch in Detective Van Slyde's temporary office at the Brambles Hotel when the alert came that the 7-Eleven just north of Pacific Palisades had been robbed.

Officer Jones opened the door to the office.

"You got the call for the 7-Eleven?" he asked. "They're short-staffed at the station tonight."

"Are you taking the call?"

"I'm headed there now," Officer Jones said. "When do you go off duty?"

"I'll be here." Van Slyde checked his phone. "I'm not leaving until we get some results."

"I've got something from one of the domestic staff I interviewed just now," Officer Jones said.

"Tell me."

"She'd seen a woman today who used to work here, and this woman went on maternity leave about three months ago but the baby died."

"Okay."

"You told me to tell you everything I heard whether it seemed important or not."

"Of course," Detective Van Slyde said. "I meant it."

"She tried to chat with the woman, who was nervous and skittered away and disappeared."

"That's all?"

"That's all the information she had. One of the questions we were asking the staff was did you see anything out of the ordinary today, and that's what she said." He checked his notebook. "Her name is Mary Coin and *skittered* is my word, not hers."

"The domestic you interviewed is Mary Coin?"

"Yes."

"But you didn't get the name of the former employee?"

"She didn't remember the name, but since she was on maternity leave, I'm sure the hotel could identify her. See you later." He closed the door behind him.

"What about Jess?" Teddy asked after Officer Jones left for the 7-Eleven.

Detective Van Slyde rested his hand on her arm.

"Baby Ruby can't talk and move on her own, so the LAPD is focusing a lot of their search on Jess right now and hoping she and Baby Ruby might be in the same place."

"Me too," Teddy said. "That's what I'm hoping."

"I am going to need to depend on you here. We need as much information as you can give us and I count on the fact that you're levelheaded."

Levelheaded!

Her parents would be astonished to hear that. No one had ever called her levelheaded before.

Teddy's phone rang and she reached into her back pocket.

"Your sister?" Detective Van Slyde asked quickly.

Teddy looked at the phone and shook her head.

"My mother," she said.

"Teddy!" Delilah said, loud enough that her voice filled the small office. "Where are you?"

"In the office where Detective Van Slyde is working."

"He still hasn't a clue about Jess or Baby Ruby?"

"I don't think so, Mom."

"I'm coming down, okay?"

Teddy looked at Detective Van Slyde, who nodded, reaching out for the phone.

"You can certainly come down, Mrs. O'Fines. Just understand that we are working on every lead we get and, though we haven't found her yet, we're not going to bed until we do."

Van Slyde was a tall, large man, flushed in the cheeks, with big hands, a soft belly, and a wide, generous smile. He gave the phone back to Teddy and leaned over, his elbows resting on his knees, his hands folded, and spoke quietly.

"Tell me about Jess."

"She's the good girl in the family," Teddy said. "The *do everything you're asked to do* girl. She gets good grades and doesn't complain. We call her the Save-the-Marriage Baby because she's the baby my parents had in order to save their marriage."

"If you were to guess, what do you imagine she might be doing right now?"

"I am pretty sure she's trying to find Baby Ruby herself."

Teddy told Detective Van Slyde again about the small man in the bright green shirt that Jess had seen just before Baby Ruby disappeared.

"The man saw Jess holding Ruby. He was walking in her direction when she closed the door. The same man she chased through the lobby, down the steps into the parking garage, and lost."

"I have that in my notes."

"And then there was the woman hiding in the linen closet and smelling of rosemary," Teddy said.

"Rosemary?"

"Jess is an amazing sniffer."

Teddy pulled her knees up under her chin.

"There's another thing," she said. "After my parents were divorced and it was only Jess and me at home, my mother wanted to find a new husband, so she was out a lot at night. So Jess and I had a detective agency and we, especially Jess, imagined crimes. After school, we would solve the crime and find the criminal. Jess was excellent at this game."

"So you think she has taken matters into her own hands?"

"I do," Teddy said. "I think that when I lost touch with her it was because she saw maybe the man whom she followed through the garage, or else the woman she saw in the linen closet. She's fearless, Jess."

"You'd recognize the man?"

"I think so. He looks like a boy. A black-haired sort of soft-faced boy."

"I'll add that to the description."

"Also," Teddy said, feeling the need to tell this detective the truth, "I should tell you that I live in a home for girls in trouble because I'm a shoplifter."

Detective Van Slyde's expression did not change at all, his blue eyes warm as the sea.

"You are?"

She nodded.

"That's not the worst thing," he said. "Shoplifting is against the law but it doesn't hurt anyone," he said. "I am in the business of finding people who hurt other people. You're an exceptional young woman, Teddy. You'll get over shoplifting."

Tears were spilling down Teddy's cheeks as the door to the office opened and Delilah was there.

"I don't know what's going on here, but you must be on vacation, Detective Van Slyde."

"I can tell you what little we know so far. Nothing confirmed, of course, except that it appears your daughter, Jess, has taken matters into her own hands and she still isn't answering her cell phone."

~

Jess woke up when the car stopped and the music was turned off.

"There's someone in the 7-Eleven," Angel said from the backseat.

"I see her. She's buying milk and walking to the cash register. So she'll pay and leave with her milk and then, unless somebody else comes, I'll have a little time."

"Be careful."

"I've never robbed a store. I don't know what *be careful* means."

"The person at the cash register looks like a boy. He's probably younger than sixteen, so as long as no one else is working there . . ."

The door opened and Jess could feel the driver's seat empty. In the backseat, Angel was whimpering.

"Here comes the woman with her milk," Angel said. "Act casual, like you're just doing an errand."

But there was no answer.

The whimpering stopped.

"He's in the store now," she said. "Can you hear me, girl?"

Jess lay very still. She had a cramp in her leg and was counting over and over again — 1, 2, 3, 4, 5, 6, 7, 8, 9, 10, 1, 2, 3, 4 — to distract herself.

"Of course you can hear me. I know you," Angel said. "I saw you in the linen closet a few hours ago and you saw me. We spoke."

Angel was silent for a moment, but nervous. Jess could tell by the short, fast breaths she took, the tiny birdsong in her throat.

"Jack's looking at the magazines," she said. "I don't know why he's spending time looking at the magazines when someone could come in any second. Now he's gone to the counter and the boy is handing him a pack of cigarettes from behind the counter and he's getting his money out of his pocket and, oh my god, I can't look."

She was whimpering again.

Jess kept counting and it helped. She didn't think about the cramp if she kept counting, didn't miss a beat, but if her mind wandered just for a second, the pain was unbearable and she wanted to jump out of her skin.

"Oh no, oh my god," Angel whispered from the backseat, and then the door opened and he was back in the driver's seat — the smell of him was cigarettes and something sweet — Jess didn't recognize the smell, maybe coconut, stronger than it had been before. The car was in reverse, the squeaking sound of rubber tires, a right turn, and they were moving at a regular speed.

"Why don't you drive faster?" Angel asked.

"Why drive faster and call attention to ourselves? Maybe get arrested for speeding. Now that wouldn't be too smart, would it, Angel."

"Did you get the money?"

"Weren't you watching me?"

"I was too scared to watch."

"I got the money. It was quite easy and the boy was a wimp. I grabbed him around the shoulders, gagged him, dropped with him to the ground so we weren't visible behind the counter, tied his arms and legs. The cash register was open, so I took all the bills — a ton of bills — and skipped the change and left."

"Now what?"

"Now someone will come into the 7-Eleven any moment — the 7-Eleven is busy around here on a Friday night and I was very lucky —

they'll see the boy behind the counter, ungag him, untie him, and call the police. When the police come he'll give them a description of me — probably the boy didn't see the car — he's not the sharpest tack in the drawer — so we need to go somewhere pronto."

"Venice Beach," Angel said. "A lot of cars, a lot of people. No one will notice."

"I don't think so, Angel. I don't think you're a very good criminal."

"Then where?"

"We're going back to your sister's, around back, park in the space behind her house, and count the money."

"What about the girl?"

There was a long silence and in the front of the car, her face pressed into the carpet, her eyes wide open, Jess stopped counting. Would she have a chance to talk to them? She was good at talking. She could save herself by talking. And did they have it in mind to hurt her or take her with them? And for what reason would they take her with them? Better to dump her somewhere dark where no one would see her until the morning light. They probably wouldn't take out the gag or untie her, but if they did, she would talk. She would congratulate Jack for robbing the 7-Eleven, tell him how clever and capable he was at robbery; that her sister was also a robber, but of things, not money; she would tell them that they were not *bad* people, not criminals, at least. Only people who needed something they didn't have, and she wondered, it had just crossed her mind, if what they wanted was a baby.

"So what about the girl?"

"We'll dump the girl," he said, taking a left turn and then a right, slowing to a stop.

"She'll be able to identify you when the police talk to her."

"I won't be around to identify, Angel, and nor will you."

"Why do you think no one will find us?"

"We'll be in Kansas."

"Kansas?"

"The girl has ears, Angel, so do you think with her in the car, knowing what's going on, I'll tell the truth about where we're going?"

The car turned, probably into a driveway, and the engine turned off.

"Don't turn the light on inside the car," Angel said. "Someone will see us."

"I have a flashlight so I'm counting the money, and if there's enough, I'm heading in the house to pay your sister. Did you notice the light is on in her bedroom?"

There was a long silence except for the ruffle of paper and Jess rubbing her face against the carpet.

"Done," he said.

"How much?"

"Eight hundred and twenty-five dollars," he said. "I have plenty in my wallet to make up the difference."

The car door opened.

"Scrunch down, Angel. I don't want anyone driving by to see you."

CHAPTER FOURTEEN

FOUR A.M. IN ROOM 618

Delilah insisted on a meeting in room 618 with her family and Detective Van Slyde.

"As far as I can see, we're getting nowhere," Delilah said to Detective Van Slyde as they went up in the elevator. Teddy, her eyes closed, her head resting against the mirror, had her hands over her ears. Her mother was making her sick.

"From our point of view, we have small but not insignificant leads," Van Slyde said.

"It's all conversation," Delilah said. "No baby has been heard from and the only thing I'm interested in is Ruby."

"And Jess," Teddy said.

Even with her hands over her ears, she was unable to close out her mother's voice.

"Of course, Jess. Jess . . ." Her voice thinned to a ribbon of sound as she spoke her daughter's name.

Delilah called Danny to alert him that they were coming upstairs for a conference, and NO there was NO news about Baby Ruby and Jess was MIA.

"Missing in Action," Delilah added.

"Do we have to do this, Mom?" Danny asked.

"We have to do EVERYTHING we can possibly do."

When they opened the door, Whee was lying on the bed, a pillow over her face, in jeans and a T-shirt and bare feet.

"She's getting married tomorrow," Delilah said to Van Slyde.

"I'm not getting married tomorrow." Whee's voice was matter-of-fact.

Beet had shut herself in the bathroom and asked not to be disturbed.

"They had a fight," Victor told Delilah in a stage whisper, indicating the bathroom door. He was sitting at the end of the bed next to Whee's feet. "Danny and Beet."

"Tension is very high in here, Delilah," Aldie said. "Probably not a good idea to have the police at this moment."

"Too late," Delilah said. "The police ARE here."

"We're a peace-loving family and never fight," Aldie said apologetically. "But we're all so upset about Jess and Baby Ruby that we're taking it out on each other."

"I would just like to know what you guys have found out so far," Danny asked the officer who followed Delilah through the door.

"We've come up to get your help if you can give it," Van Slyde said.

"Officer, we know nothing at all," Aldie said. "We left Jess in charge of the baby while we went downstairs in the hotel for the rehearsal dinner and came back to find the baby and Jess missing. That's the full extent of information we have."

"We have no more *confirmed* information than that," Detective Van Slyde said, standing next to the door, his arms folded across his chest. Teddy was beside him, leaning against the wall. Her eyes were closed so she didn't have to witness her family's crazy sadness. "But we have some *unconfirmed* information and we could use your help as we try to follow Jess and what action she might have taken to find the baby. It would be helpful to have your conjecture on what she might do in this situation."

"I have no intelligence on Jess," Danny said. "I expected her to be able to take care of a four-month-old baby and I guessed wrong."

"You forgot to get a babysitter knowing that, of course, Jess would do it," Teddy said. She could not help herself. "Jess had no choice."

"Enough," Aldie said. "Go ahead, Officer."

"We know — and it may mean nothing at all — but a former member of the hotel domestic staff, who left because she was pregnant and lost the baby, has been seen at the hotel with a well-dressed man who may be her boyfriend. This is the kind of lead we follow," Detective Van Slyde said. "It may take us to a dead end. And it may not."

The door to the bathroom opened and Beet stood in the semidarkness.

"What are you saying?" she asked the detective.

"I am trying to construct a possible story since all we have are hints. Leads that we follow until we discover whether they make sense or not."

"Is that all the story you have?"

"We know that Jess followed a well-dressed man who she thought may have been the one to take the baby, followed him into the garage where he'd gone to get his car, and then she lost him. Teddy believes that the man *knew* Jess was following him and that he recognized her from the sixth floor."

"And we know that Jess is gone. Zilch!" Delilah said. "That's the whole story."

"We locked down the hotel at eleven fifteen tonight, which is the procedure when there has been a criminal event, in order to question as many people as possible and to keep anyone from leaving or entering."

"So have you found anything out?"

"Nothing conclusive but we do know that a member of the hotel staff saw a girl meeting Jess's description leave the hotel just before lockdown."

"This is absurd," Beet said, her voice breaking.

She slipped back into the dark bathroom and closed the door.

"You are suggesting that a member of the cleaning staff had a baby and the baby died," Delilah was saying, "and then today she came back to the hotel with her well-dressed boyfriend to steal some poor baby who happened to be staying as a guest."

Delilah had moved across the room and was now sitting on the bed next to Victor.

"That is a possible story. All we know is the information about the staff member on maternity leave. Nothing else."

"It makes very little sense," Delilah said.

"I'm making a story out of the few facts we have to determine if we can fill in the blanks," Detective Van Slyde said. "I could be completely wrong, of course, but this is the way we follow a lead."

"Well, if you want to know what Jess is doing, ask Teddy. Teddy is the only member of the family she talks to," Delilah said.

"I've already told him that I *knew* Jess would follow the man if she ever saw him again," Teddy said. "And if she found the woman who was hiding in the sixth-floor linen closet, she'd follow her too."

"This sounds like hokeypokey just to quiet us down."

"Of course it may be just hokeypokey," Detective Van Slyde said, reaching in his pocket where his phone was ringing.

"Yes?" he said.

He looked over at Teddy and gave her a thumbs-up.

"No kidding? At four o'clock in the morning? Who's around then?"

There was a long pause.

"Where? Yup, good news and thanks."

He put his phone back in his pocket.

"That was Officer Jones. Jess's cell was found by someone changing a flat tire on the highway going north of Santa Monica just before Pacific Palisades. It's at the station now."

Jess waited, listening to Angel's breathing — long breaths followed by a sigh. Something was about to happen. She could feel it in the dank air stinking of motor oil, in Angel no longer whimpering in the backseat. It seemed like hours — the ties around her wrists cutting into her skin — before anything happened, and then the car door opened.

"Shhhh," he said. "We're leaving."

Jess heard a woman's voice, not Angel's.

"Here's your package," the woman said.

The man climbed into the front seat, turned on the engine, then a car door again, a slip of air around Jess's face.

"Maria was fine," the man said. "I gave her a thousand."

"No other requests?"

"For what? A thousand is plenty."

The car backed up, turned quickly enough to roll Jess into the door, and then headed forward at a reasonable pace. They drove for a while, city driving, stop start, red lights, stop signs, and then they were on the highway, the pace increasing.

"Jack, when?"

"Soon," he replied.

What would happen *soon*? Jess wondered. Would they kill her? Throw her into the ocean, tied like she was so she would drown? Was she frightened? she asked herself, thinking that of course she was frightened, her heart in her throat, her breath thin. But she wasn't frightened to death. If she had thought of this moment while safe under her covers at home, she would have imagined it so terrifying she couldn't survive. And *this* moment did not feel like the end of her life.

The car felt different than it had felt before Jack had gone into the house with money for Maria. For one thing, Angel wasn't whimpering in the way she had been — she seemed to be humming deep in her throat. Jess heard a sound behind her, a kind of mewing, and then Jack turned the music on again, but softly.

"Do you know what we're doing?" Angel asked from the backseat.

"I know we're not going to talk about it in front of the girl," he said. "That much I know, Angel, and I hope you'll pay attention."

"I mean what we're doing about the girl?"

"Count on it. I'm going to do something about the girl."

"Okay," she said, humming again, and Jack turned the music up.

Jess had no sense of time except even through her blindfold, she sensed the night was fading. Lightening, not light, so maybe it was coming on morning. Certainly the drive was going on and on forever without any more conversation, only the low sound of Angel in the backseat.

Her family would be desperate — the baby gone, now Jess, no chance without Jess of finding the baby. Maybe no chance of finding her even with Jess's help. Just the police in room 618 at the Brambles, and Delilah hysterical like Danny was hysterical, and Whee lying on the bed still as stone. Victor thinking maybe he should bolt. Aldie taking charge, maybe even grateful for this opportunity to be the man of the family again.

Terrible things would be said about Jess. Of that she was certain, especially from Danny and Delilah. Irresponsible. Selfish. Foolish. Childish. Self-involved. That's what they said about Teddy's shoplifting. Self-involved. Of course she was self-involved. Who in the world wasn't?

Thinking of Teddy made her less frightened. Maybe stronger, maybe simply important enough not to die on this highway in California.

The car slowed, turned, the road now bumpy. They came to a stop.

"Where are we?" Angel asked.

Jack didn't reply.

"Do you know where we are?"

"Of course I know, Angel."

The car door opened and Jess could sense him getting out. Then another car door, the blanket removed, and Jess was lifted out, gently, she thought later. He put her down on hard ground. Earth, not asphalt.

"Sorry, kid," he said.

The car door shut again, a revving of the engine, and she could hear the car moving away, a bumpy road. Then racing along asphalt until it was only a low purr in the distance.

So — she thought, relieved. She had not been killed. She had not been injured. She was lying somewhere in the real world, a living girl with rope burns on her arms and legs and an empty belly roaring with hunger. Sometime, maybe even in the early daylight, someone would find *her*.

But not Baby Ruby. She had failed Baby Ruby, and the hot tears spilled through the cloth over her eyes and down her cheeks.

CHAPTER FIFTEEN

BY THE LIGHT OF DAY

Jess's cell phone was found on the highway, on the right bank of the road headed north before Pacific Palisades. It lay on the soft earth lining the asphalt. While the man who discovered it was changing his flat tire, he heard it ringing. The phone was dented at the top, probably where it initially hit the asphalt. Then it must have bounced to the edge of the highway.

There were seventeen messages, all from Teddy.

Tears of relief gathered behind Teddy's eyes.

That the phone was discovered, that it still worked, and that the glass wasn't shattered was a sign. *A good sign*, she thought, willing herself not to think about the worst.

"So this is good?" she asked Van Slyde.

"That we found the phone is good but not important. It's *where* we found the phone that is helpful."

"So?" Danny asked.

"Daniel." Aldie's voice had an authority Teddy had rarely heard in her father. "The police are not trying to annoy you. It's very important to work with them."

"We're dispatching police all over the area," Van Slyde said. "We assume that Jess was in a car headed north and that someone, probably not Jess, threw the phone out the window of the moving car."

"So you do think there's a connection between Jess's disappearance and Baby Ruby," Delilah asked quietly. "Is that your thought, Detective Van Slyde?"

"That's the thought we're going with now that we have a tangible clue," Van Slyde said. "The phone and a defined geography. That is why several cars have been dispatched to comb the area. I am going to check it out."

"They could both be dead, of course, and all we'll be left with is the cell phone," Danny said.

The bathroom door opened and Beet leaned out.

"Don't talk anymore, Danny."

"I was just saying . . ."

"I mean, don't talk at all," Beet said. "You are making me sick."

Van Slyde turned to go.

"Are you leaving now?" Teddy asked.

"Now and quickly. I'm following up on the cell phone."

"I want to come," Teddy said.

"With me?" Detective Van Slyde said. "I don't think so, Teddy."

"Please, I need to go. If we find her, and we will, Jess would want me there."

"It's not safe, Ted," Delilah said. "Is it safe, Detective Van Slyde?"

"There are risks, certainly. These people are criminals — they have two children they've kidnapped, at least we assume that is where Jess is. And we don't know whether they're armed. We do have information on the employee who lost a baby and may be involved — but that's not definite and her reputation at the Brambles was good. Nevertheless."

"I'll do everything you ask me to do, Detective Van Slyde. Everything. I won't take any risks. Please. I'll be helpful, especially with Jess."

"Okay," Van Slyde said. "I will let her come if you agree. She could be helpful."

"No," Delilah said.

"Let her go, Delilah," Aldie said. "These two girls know each other very well, and who knows how Teddy can help."

In the elevator, Van Slyde was silent.

"Thank you," Teddy said.

They walked across the lobby, through the doors, and into his police car parked on the circle.

"Where are we going now?" she asked. "To the police station?"

"There is reason to assume that the phone was thrown from a car and Jess was in that car," he said.

"This is my first time in California and I don't have any idea where things are, like the airport."

"What you *do* know is your sister and you can be very helpful with that."

"How do you mean?" Teddy asked.

"So let's say Jess is in the car with the kidnapper, maybe with the baby, maybe not. But with the person who kidnapped the baby."

"She's probably blindfolded so she won't be able to identify the kidnappers," Teddy said. "And Baby Ruby will be crying her head off. That's the kind of baby she is."

There was traffic, surprising for the middle of the night, and Teddy had a sense that it was coming on morning. Something eerie about the night — damp, cloudy, no stars in sight, a pale, ghostly sliver of moon on the horizon. The cars seemed to be floating down the highway.

"Jess would be practical," Teddy said. "In an emergency, she's calm, like my dad, who goes into slow motion when there's a problem. But not slow motion without thinking. She will be trying to put things together. She'll be afraid, but not scared to death."

"That's good," Detective Van Slyde said. "No hysterics. Hysterics get in the way of common sense."

A disembodied voice coming from the police radio filled the inside of the car.

"Van Slyde?"

"Here," he said.

"Where are you?"

"Just by Pacific Palisades."

"Do you have a description of the baby?"

"Did you find her?" Teddy asked, her heart beating in her throat.

"We just need a detailed description."

Van Slyde reached over and touched Teddy's arm.

"Repeat the description for the officer."

"She's four months old, with red-and-yellow hair, sort of golden, in circles around her head, like it's going to be curly. And she has a dimple on the right side of her mouth and a little brown birthmark in the middle of her forehead, sort of beigy brown in the shape of a pear, and her feet, her little feet are skinny and long for a baby. So are her hands. And, I almost forgot, she has webbed toes, two of them webbed together on her right foot."

"Good," Detective Van Slyde said.

"Thank you," the voice said. There was a pause and then he went on.

"Paul?"

"Yes."

"Keep heading north."

So his name was Paul. Detective Paul Van Slyde.

"You should know we had a call from Venice Beach," the voice on the radio said. "A neighbor reported that a car pulled up to a house and a woman, big, athletic woman, in a long skirt and a halter top, came out the back door of her place with a baby and slid the baby through the car window of a stopped car that had a man in the driver's seat."

"Okay," Van Slyde said.

"The neighbor called the police because he'd heard the alert about the baby on the radio."

"Interesting."

"Someone has been dispatched to the address of the neighbor to check it out."

"Long shot, but maybe," Van Slyde said.

"Now what?" Teddy asked.

"Now we're just about at the place where the phone was found, so if we head up the highway another half mile, that's the spot."

"Then we'll go to Venice Beach?"

"I'm just following instincts and waiting for more word from the station."

He pulled off the highway, stopped the car, and got out.

"This is where they found your sister's cell phone," he said. "Don't get out."

He walked up and down the grass strip, where another police car was parked. Teddy watched him, watched him talk to another officer for a second, watched him stop, kneel down on his haunches observing the traffic, and then get back in the police car.

"What did you see?" Teddy asked.

"Nothing," he replied. "I was watching the traffic to see how fast it was going and whether a phone thrown from a window at that speed would have shattered, or whether they might have slowed down or even pulled over to the side of the road and dropped the phone, which then hit the asphalt and bounced away off the road."

"Does it make a difference?"

"Probably not. It's a way of thinking."

"I know about that way of thinking," Teddy said. "We had this game."

"You told me."

"I'm glad we're going to the house where the woman put a baby in the car."

"Don't get your hopes up."

"Isn't it strange to slip a baby through a half-opened window like that?"

"We don't know who was in the car."

"I just want to think that this is important."

Detective Van Slyde turned on the engine but didn't immediately pull back onto the highway. His hands on the steering wheel, his eyes checked the rearview mirror.

"Now?" Teddy asked. "Venice Beach?"

"Not yet," he said, pulling back onto the highway, into the middle lane, accelerating and heading north.

"So?"

"So the car was headed north. Otherwise, we would not have found the phone on the right side of the road, correct?"

"Correct."

Teddy felt a shiver of excitement.

"And your sister was in the car. We must assume she was in the car or they wouldn't have headed north with just her cell phone, right?"

"I think so."

"So I'm guessing they were traveling this road on their way north out of Los Angeles or maybe planning to go inland. With your sister or not."

"It's been a while since they found the phone, right?" Teddy asked.

"If they *are* ahead of us, that's about an hour ahead, and it's possible, if they are driving fast, they might have driven a long way."

"Or they could have decided that they didn't want Jess in the car any longer and dumped her."

"Why would they dump her since she could identify them?"

"Not if she was blindfolded." Teddy drew her knees up and rested her chin. "Except . . ." she began.

"Except," Detective Van Slyde said. "If it was the same man she had seen in the corridor on the sixth floor, then she could already identify them."

"Right. But maybe he wanted to dump her and then drive inland out of town. Maybe Baby Ruby was in the trunk of the car."

"Let's hope not," Detective Van Slyde said.

Ahead on the highway, to the right, there was a lot of commotion: two police cars, a truck pulled over to the side of the road, people standing just off the asphalt, sirens in the far distance.

"Ambulance," Van Slyde said.

"Is it an accident?"

"Looks that way."

They drove up to the back of a crowd of people, cars, a fire truck, the two police cars, and more on the way. The sound of the ambulance came closer.

Detective Van Slyde pulled the car to a stop.

"I don't want to look," Teddy said. "I'll throw up."

"Good idea to stay in the car, then," he said. "I'll only be a minute."

He got out of the car and headed to the crowd. Teddy, her head down, closed her eyes and waited.

Waited and waited but Van Slyde did not come back. The ambulance arrived. Two men got out and headed just beyond her line of vision. Policemen gathered in a huddle but Teddy couldn't make out what it was they were watching. Then the men from the ambulance returned, opened the back door, and took out a stretcher.

Behind them, Teddy saw Paul Van Slyde walking back toward the car.

She was huddled in the front seat when he opened the car door.

"Are you okay?" he asked.

She nodded.

"It's not an accident," he said. "Come with me."

—~—

Jess lay very still, twisting her wrists back and forth. If she was calm, she thought, if she didn't permit herself to be so frantic, then maybe she could slowly get free. But only if she didn't get impatient.

The rope was thin, not twine but more like wire, and would not budge. On her stomach, she tossed her head back and forth against the ground, hoping to dislodge the blindfold. It felt tight on her head but it was cloth, soft cloth, so she ought to be able to move it.

The gray light of early dawn slipped in under the cloth and Jess was conscious of where she was, what was around her: a large field with high grass, a big sky, the highway. Almost as if she could actually see. There were a lot of cars on the highway. The speed of traffic drowned out any other sound. She stopped struggling and lay very still. Thinking. That was what she used to do when she played SLEUTH with Teddy. Think and imagine what terrible crime might have taken place and how had it happened and who was responsible.

Where had Angel and Jack gone when they dropped her? Did they kidnap Baby Ruby as she certainly believed they had done? Or had the coincidence of the small man coming toward room 618 and the stealing of Baby Ruby been only a coincidence? If Angel and Jack were the ones who had taken Ruby, where was the baby? At Angel's sister's house or lost or even in the car with Jess? If she had been in the car, why hadn't Jess heard her whimpering?

She was becoming less desperate.

She thought about what she now knew that she had not known before Jack had dragged her into the car.

What got said between Angel and Jack while Jess was tied up in the car had to do with babies. There was the sister, Maria, who asked to be paid a lot of money for a favor. A thousand dollars. And what was the favor?

There was Angel weeping and weeping. Something about a baby and the cemetery.

If only she could see them face-to-face and tell them how sorry she was about what happened.

"I'm so sorry for whatever terrible thing happened to you," she would say to Angel.

Then she would ask them where Baby Ruby had been taken.

Would they tell Jess? Or were they going to ask for money to give the baby back?

Jess was beginning to get sleepy when she heard the scream of brakes. A car pulled up very close to where she was lying.

A door slammed.

"Jake?"

It was a man's voice.

"I was right, Jake," he went on. "It's a body."

"Coming!" another man said. Probably Jake.

"A girl," the first man said. "Tied up. She isn't dead."

"Well, I'll be darned, Buddy," the man, Jake, said softly.

"A girl."

"Right here near the highway for anyone to see her."

Buddy leaned down and untied the blindfold, took out the rag stuffed into Jess's mouth, almost halfway down her throat. Her mouth was as dry as sandpaper.

She could actually see.

The men were young, maybe twenty, maybe a little older, both bearded with longish hair, one dark, the other — the man called Jake — very blond with a short, square beard and glasses. They smelled of alcohol.

Jake untied the ropes around her ankles and wrists and lifted her to her feet.

"Jeez," he said. "You're wobbly. How long have you been tied up?"

"Long," Jess said. "All night. The ties were really tight."

The dark-haired scruffy man, Buddy, stood back and looked at Jess.

"Are you okay?" he asked.

Jess nodded.

"Can you talk?"

Her tongue seemed to have expanded to fill her mouth.

"I think I can." She was tentative.

"So what happened?"

She spoke slowly, as if she had a wad of cotton in her mouth, but she *could* speak.

"I was tied up and blindfolded and driven around in a car by two people who I'd seen before but didn't know."

"Just tied up for no particular reason and left on the edge of the highway?"

"There was a reason," she said. "I was babysitting and Ruby was on the floor of our hotel room and I went into the bathroom to try on my sister's wedding dress and then someone kidnapped my baby niece."

"That's a lot of information," Jake said.

"So they kidnapped you?" Buddy said.

"More or less."

"Call the police," Jake said.

"Are you crazy, Jake? We've been drinking. We'll be arrested."

"This is more important, Buddy. Just call them."

"Where do I tell them we are?"

"About a mile south of Pacific Palisades on the right shoulder going north. Tell them we have this kid."

"How old are you?" Buddy asked.

"Twelve."

"And you live around here?"

"I live in Larchmont, New York."

"Larchmont, New York. Never heard of it."

The dark-haired man put his hand on her shoulder and led her to their truck, opened the door, and lifted her into the passenger seat. "You must be hungry," he said.

"Sort of."

"All we have is cashews and M&M's."

"Beer!"

"Make sense, Jake. Don't bring up the beer."

"Were you scared?" Buddy asked.

"A little," she said. "Could I have the cashews?"

Jake bit the package of cashews with his teeth, turned Jess's hand over, and poured cashews into her palm.

"You're a pretty chill girl," Buddy said. "I'm impressed."

"How long do you think you've been here?" Jake asked.

"Not very long. The man lifted me out of the car. He was kind of nice."

"Real nice," Jake said. "Tie you up, blindfold you, gag you. A really great guy."

"He said 'Sorry, kid' when he left, like he meant it. That's what I mean by nice."

"So we're calling the police, is that okay?"

"It's okay. They already know about Baby Ruby."

Buddy dialed 911.

Just short of Pacific Palisades going north, he told them.

"So we'll cool our heels and the emergency teams should be here soon."

—〜—

The sirens, off in the distance, were coming from the south and the north, screaming into the sunrise.

Jess put her hands over her ears.

"You're a big deal," Jake said. "Listen to that noise. They've sent the whole Los Angeles police force. Ambulances, fire engines, probably the bomb squad out to get you. One little girl with that much power."

Jess's eyes filled with tears.

There were the flashing lights of an ambulance, two police cars, and then more coming from the north, and a fire engine, although there was no fire. And then the police, and the ambulance driver and the paramedic, and a fireman hopping out of the front seat, all converging on the truck belonging to Jake and Buddy, and on Jess O'Fines sitting in the passenger seat, her hands folded in her lap, tears pouring down her cheeks.

"It's the girl who disappeared. The one who'd been watching the baby," one officer said. "Your name?" he asked.

"Jess O'Fines."

"And what are you doing here?"

Jess told him the story as the other officers gathered around, a crowd around her — "like you're famous," Jake said, patting her on the back.

"And these gentlemen?"

"They saved me," Jess said.

"Jake Brown."

"Buddy Brown. We're brothers and we were driving up to Topanga and saw this body of a girl lying so close to the highway we could see her, so we stopped."

"And took off my blindfold and untied the rope around my legs and wrists and took out the gag in my mouth."

"And do you know who did this to you?"

"I do," Jess said.

"And you could identify them?"

"I could identify the man and I am sure I know the woman although I didn't see her when the man dragged me into the car and tied me up," she said. "I had seen her earlier at the hotel. She had this rosemary smell."

"Rosemary?"

Jess nodded. "That's how I knew it was her."

He shrugged and she told him about the woman crouched in the corner of the sixth-floor linen closet of the Brambles Hotel and how she smelled of rosemary, just like the woman smelling of rosemary in the backseat of the car she had been in.

"We have the background of this story," the officer who was questioning Jess said to the others who had gathered around. "A baby girl was taken from the Brambles Hotel last night while this young lady was babysitting her. Detective Van Slyde in my station is on this case."

"It was my fault," Jess said. "Also, you should know that the man and the woman in the car were not unkind. When the man took me out of the car and put me on the ground, he said 'Sorry, kid,' as if he were really sorry."

Light was beginning to spread over the horizon, coming on morning, the day of Whee's wedding, the day for which the O'Fineses had been waiting all year.

And now this.

She could not imagine what was happening with her family right now. Where they were and what they were saying about Jess and whether they would ever want to see her again in their lives.

"Hey, Paul," the officer taking notes called out and then he turned to Jess.

"Here comes Van Slyde," he said, "and he's probably got something to tell us."

Jess looked across the field where the highway met the high grasses.

Her breath caught in her throat.

It was Teddy. Teddy coming through the dawn light in Jess's direction.

CHAPTER SIXTEEN

SLEUTH LLC

Jess and Teddy climbed into the back of Van Slyde's patrol car and held hands. Neither spoke.

"I thought you might be dead," Teddy said finally.

"I didn't think — I mean most of the time I didn't think that something awful would happen to me."

"Was it incredibly scary?"

"Being tied up, especially with a gag, was scary. But I'm okay. I'm pretty much fine."

"Fine, I bet." Teddy threw her arms around her sister. "So tell me everything."

And Jess did, starting at the beginning when she was following Angel and got pulled inside the car.

Detective Van Slyde did a U-turn heading south.

"Okay, girls. We're headed to Venice Beach," he said. "I don't have time to take you to Santa Monica and Jess especially can help us on this. At least you heard the voices of the kidnappers and can identify them."

"To Venice Beach," Teddy said to Jess. "That's where they think Ruby might have been seen."

"Are you doing okay back there?" he called.

"Fine," Jess said. "We're good."

"We're going to meet another squad car and get some information," he said. "So tell me what you know, Jess."

"What I know is that I was tied up and gagged and blindfolded so I didn't see anything. I just heard things and what I heard was from the two people, a man and a woman, Jack and Angel. Jack was in the front seat and I was on the floor by the passenger seat, Angel was in the back and they were getting out of town, maybe with a baby, and maybe that baby was in the car after Jack delivered the money to Angel's sister, whose name is Maria. Usually it was Angel whimpering, but after we stopped at Maria's and before I was taken out of the car, I heard a different whimpering sound, like a kitten."

"How did you end up in the car in the first place?" he asked.

"I was walking along the line of cars and taxis by the hotel and a man reached out and pulled me in the car."

"And you know the baby wasn't in the car then."

"If there was a baby, it wasn't Ruby."

"Ruby cries a lot," Teddy added.

"Also, they talked about another baby, who seems to be in the cemetery, and then we stopped someplace after Jack robbed the 7-Eleven. He had to rob the 7-Eleven of a thousand dollars to get the money to pay Maria for something that had to do with a baby. Angel cried a lot."

"So you overheard quite a bit."

"I know — at least I think I know — that the man is the same one I saw at the hotel on the sixth floor and who I chased in the garage."

"And what about the woman?"

"She was the one who smelled of rosemary."

"They're married?"

"I don't know," Jess said. "They fought."

"How did they treat you?" Van Slyde asked.

"They were nice to me, especially the man."

"Do you think he could have been armed?"

"You mean with a gun?" Jess asked.

"With a gun."

She had never thought he would have a gun, had not even been afraid that he was armed with a weapon at all. The only terror she had was to be thrown in the ocean with the gag and blindfold and rope around her ankles and wrists. But everything moved quickly and the smell at the bottom of the car was so strong that she didn't have time to worry about her future.

"They didn't seem like criminals," Jess said.

"Why not?" Teddy asked.

"I don't know," she said. "They seemed too upset and like ordinary people to be criminals."

"Because they were afraid of being caught?" Detective Van Slyde asked.

"Maybe," Jess said. "But what they really seemed upset about was something else."

"Like what?" Van Slyde asked.

"We went to a cemetery because of a baby and Angel cried a lot. It drove Jack a little crazy."

"So we're headed to this house where we have a report a baby was put in a car tonight. One of the neighbors who had been listening to the radio report of Ruby's disappearance called in that report."

The squad car slowed and they turned left away from the ocean down a narrow street almost too thin for a car.

"I don't know if we were here before. They drove all over the place," Jess said. "I wouldn't have known even without a blindfold, but I know we stopped at the sister's house."

They pulled up to a small pink cottage and Van Slyde got out.

"I'm going to break with one more protocol and ask you to come with me, Jess. Just hold back, not up on the porch," he said. "I'm interested if anything about the woman is familiar to you."

"Only her voice would be," Jess said. "And I don't even know about that."

The garden in front of the pink house was illuminated and full of flowers. There was a statue of Jesus or St. Francis of Assisi, and birdhouses and little decorative frogs, and wound around hibiscus trees were flashing Christmas lights.

Jess climbed out of the backseat.

"You okay, Teddy?" she asked.

"I'm going to throw up."

"No, you're not, Ted."

"Panic attack?"

"Not that either," Jess said. "We'll be right back."

The woman stood with her arms folded across her chest, her chin up, her eyes narrowed.

"This is my property, you know," she said.

"We had a call that a woman at this address came out of the house about an hour ago," Van Slyde said. "She had a baby in her arms and handed the baby through a half-open window on the driver's side. The people in the car — or one person, maybe one in the back, the caller was not clear — drove out of this street, turning left."

"So who called?"

"Someone who saw this happen."

"Nobody comes on this street but the people who live here."

"So I guess it was someone who lives here."

"No one who lives here would do that," she said. "So what are you going to do now?"

"I'd like you to respond to my question about the baby. Did you put a baby in a car tonight?"

She paused.

"Please," Van Slyde said.

"I did do that," the woman said. "The baby was my brother's baby and I was keeping the baby while he went out on a date."

"It was three in the morning when we got the call."

"He went out on a late date. I didn't ask. Okay?" She turned, went in her house, and locked the door.

"Now what?" Jess asked as they pulled away.

"That's what I'm asking you," Van Slyde said. "We can't arrest her."

Jess leaned forward and rested her arms on the seat in front.

"I know there was a baby because Angel and her sister were talking about it, but I don't know if the baby was Ruby and I don't know if that woman with frogs in the yard is the sister."

"They were headed north when they dropped you off on the ground where we found you," he said. "Did they say anything that would give you an idea where they were headed?"

"Wherever they were going, I think they were going to drive. They talked about planes to Canada and buses and other kinds of escape. It would be hard to get out of here with a baby and without a car, but I know there were bus tickets. The sister had bought them bus tickets."

"Police are combing the area up and down the coast," Van Slyde said.

Jess wriggled next to Teddy. Even with the tension, she was so tired she could hardly feel her arms and legs.

"I think they are nearby," Jess finally said.

"How come?" Teddy asked.

"Because if they have Ruby now and they're trying to get out of town, they need Pampers and bottles and milk and a pacifier and a lot of stuff they probably don't have with them. They've been driving all night long with me in the car."

"So you don't think they had anything for the baby to eat or wear?" Teddy asked.

"I don't. I saw Angel, I think it was Angel, in the hotel. Then I walked along the curb looking into the windows of the cars. Then the guy called Jack pulled me in the car and Angel was in the backseat. They couldn't have had time to get food and stuff, right?"

"I suppose," Teddy said.

"They stopped at the 7-Eleven, where they might have picked up stuff for a baby, but he went to the 7-Eleven because it's open all night and he needed a thousand dollars for the sister, Maria, and he got it."

"We're up-to-date on that," Van Slyde said. "There was a robbery about an hour and a half ago, and the guy working there was discovered by a customer, tied up. He gave a pretty accurate description of Jack."

"Santa Monica?" Jess asked.

"Yes, it was in Santa Monica."

"So what might they do now?" Van Slyde asked.

"If that was Baby Ruby handed through the window and if the Venice lady was Maria, then they've got to escape L.A. Except they probably don't have stuff for the baby, who is probably screaming."

"I'm sure that's what they'd have to do," Teddy said. "But where?"

"So they'd go get stuff for the baby at an all-night CVS," Jess said.

Jess and Teddy, Van Slyde leading the way, got out of the squad car, parked in a strip mall just under a streetlight, and went into the CVS.

"You two can do the talking but I'm going to be right there."

The store was empty as far as they could tell. A young man with long blond hair tied back in a ponytail was standing behind the counter.

"We are looking for a short man in a rumpled green shirt who may have been here in the last hour or so," Jess said.

"We're a busy place and I don't have a thing for shirts, so I don't know."

"Getting baby stuff?" Teddy asked. "Bottles, Pampers, pacifiers, that sort of thing."

"Hmmm," he said, eyeing them with some suspicion. "Who are they? Hollywood?"

"He's a friend," Jess said, picking up packages of M&M's and crackers.

"Not an actor?"

"Actors aren't short," Teddy said.

"Actors *are* short," he said. "Most of the famous ones. I'm into actors, so I check it out. Five three. Five five. Pretty much my height."

"So maybe you saw him?" Jess asked.

"Maybe," he said. "If he's the guy I think he is, he bought all that stuff. Then he got cigarettes, two packs of them, and milk and a flashlight. He was short and sort of cute, you know."

"Do you happen to know when he left?" Jess asked. "We're hoping to catch up with him."

"Not long ago," the cashier said. "He dyed his hair blond. I could tell that under the light. Maybe half an hour ago, maybe less. He lit up when he left the store. I was watching."

Van Slyde paid for the merchandise.

"Policeman's with you, I guess?" the blond boy asked.

"He's my father," Jess said. "We're catching up with our friend."

___

They walked on, passing the patrol car, heading toward a line of parked cars, Van Slyde in the lead again.

"I can't protect you if I'm walking behind you," he said when Jess objected.

They stopped under a light and opened the pack of M&M's, filling their hands.

"I think we ought to be talking to each other like we're a couple of girls with nothing going on. So while we're walking we can check whether any of those cars is his."

"Would you know?"

"The car was small and blue, boxy, the same one that was in the garage. And it smelled."

"Maybe he's unpacking the stuff and giving Ruby a bottle," Teddy said. "Probably Ruby screamed bloody murder and he had to stop and get the bottles at CVS."

"I hope," Jess said.

For the first time, Jess was beginning to think they might find Ruby. She would be alive and fine and somewhere close in a car with Jack and Angel.

And they would find her.

Teddy and Jess. SLEUTHS LLC.

—~—

"How's everything at the hotel?"

"Better than you might think," Teddy said. "It could have been terrible but it's not."

"Like how?"

"Mom's a wreck but she's not falling apart. Not like you'd imagine. Dad is being very sensible, and Danny is — well, Danny is Danny. And Beet has actually been pretty amazing."

"And Whee?" Jess asked.

"Whee found the lipstick on her dress."

"Great," Jess said.

"She was okay about that. Mostly she's scared about Ruby."

"So they hate me."

"They won't hate you if you come back to the hotel with Baby Ruby."

"True," Jess said, reaching down and taking her sister's hand. "They will be so excited to see Ruby that they'll forget what happened."

The sun was starting to rise, and it was bringing enough light that they could see into the empty parked cars.

"Why do you think these cars have been left here all night?"

"I don't know," Jess said, straining her eyes, looking ahead at a small car toward the end of the line of cars. She thought she saw movement. Something in the front seat. She couldn't make out whether it was a person.

"Teddy." She grabbed her arm. "Look."

"Where?"

"Do you see over there in that small car? Something is moving."

Teddy grabbed her arm back. "In the driver's seat?"

"Let's go really slowly and, hush — his window might be open."

"Oh man," Teddy said. "I am so scared."

"I am going first and you can be right behind me," Van Slyde said.

Softly, moving very slowly, they slipped along the side of the next car, Jess's hand gripping her sister's.

Someone in the backseat, a dark form in the shape of a moving pile of laundry, a hand, something in the hand.

Jess closed her eyes tight for a second and the form materialized as a woman. The woman, certainly it was Angel, was holding a baby in one arm, a bottle in the other hand, and the baby — she had to be. A little fluff of hair, her legs kicking and kicking, her little hands reaching around the bottle.

Jack must have seen them coming in his side mirror, seen Van Slyde.

"Shit," he said.

"Drive," Angel said from the back. "Please, drive now, Jack."

But Van Slyde was walking up to the driver's side, his hand on the open window. He did not take out his gun.

~

At headquarters — they had to go to headquarters first so they could file a report — Jess held Baby Ruby — kissing her fuzzy hair, her cheeks, her nose, her ears, pushing the nipple of a half-full bottle of formula into her mouth.

"Do you have your cell?" Jess asked. "Call Delilah."

"I texted," Teddy said.

The man, Jack, leaned back with his head against the wall, and Angel, sitting a distance away on a bench, was sobbing quietly.

They took a statement from Jess, and another one from Teddy, and sat in the open office while Angel and Jack were questioned.

"Are you married?" Detective Van Slyde asked.

"Married," the man said.

"Did you take this baby from room 618 in the Brambles Hotel?"

"I did," he said quietly.

"What were you planning to do with her?"

"Keep her," Angel said, almost inaudibly. "Keep her for our very own."

"Keep her? Where were you going to take her?"

"Someplace. We were not sure. Canada. Maybe Nebraska."

"I had a baby," the woman said between sobs. "One month ago and it was a baby girl and she died and now she's in the cemetery and so Jack knew how sad I was and got me another baby. I wanted a baby too much."

"Maybe you'll get another baby," Teddy said quietly.

Jess sat with Ruby, her finger in Ruby's mouth so she wouldn't cry.

The woman didn't speak.

"We are very sorry," the man said. "It was wrong and I should not have done what I did but Angel was crying all the time —" He threw up his hands. "I couldn't stand it."

"I hope that you will let them go home now," Jess said as she and Teddy were leaving with Van Slyde.

In the squad car, Ruby was whimpering.

"Will you let them go home now?" Jess asked Detective Van Slyde.

He didn't reply.

"You won't, right?" Teddy asked.

"Kidnapping is a very serious crime."

"But they were so sad," Jess said. "Will they be treated like criminals?"

"They have committed a crime."

She slid down in her seat in the back, next to Teddy.

"I feel terrible," she whispered to her sister.

"I know," Teddy said. "Me too."

Dawn, the sun rising over the water in the distance, almost fully morning, as the squad pulled into the entrance to the Brambles Hotel.

"So it's today already," Teddy said.

"And we're invited to a wedding," Jess said, resting her head on her sister's shoulder.

CHAPTER SEVENTEEN

A WEDDING AFTER ALL

In 618 at the Brambles, the room was full of women and girls. Even Baby Ruby was on the bed while Beet changed her into her dress for the wedding: little white tights and Mary Jane shoes and a white, smocked dress and a hat that Ruby was not happy to be wearing.

Jess got out of the shower, wrapped a towel around her chest, and Teddy blow-dried her hair.

"You're going to look beautiful," Teddy said, and Jess smiled in spite of herself.

"Maybe you'd like to try some of my makeup, Jess?" Whee said, getting ready to shower.

"Jess already tried and rejected your makeup last night, Whee," Teddy said. "She's wearing my black mascara and wild-grape blush."

And everyone laughed. They laughed with relief that Ruby had been lost and found, and with surprising happiness that they were all together in Los Angeles for Whee's wedding and that they actually loved one another better than they knew.

Even Whee, who had moved the seed pearls on the bodice of her wedding dress so the tiny stain of lipstick was invisible.

Her family had been in the room when Jess and Teddy arrived with Baby Ruby. They sat on the bed side by side and there was a rush for the baby — Beet and Danny and Delilah. Aldie held back.

Beet took her, put her on her back, and removed her onesie and diapers to check for damage.

"Well, thank god, thank god," Beet said, pressing Ruby close to her chest. "I thought . . ."

"Don't even mention what you thought, Beet," Whee said. "We know. We all thought."

"I am so sorry," Jess said.

She had thought in the car, after the doctor had examined the baby at the police station, about what she would say when they arrived with Ruby at the hotel.

"What do you think?" she asked Teddy.

"Try me," Teddy said.

"I am sorry and ashamed. That's what I was thinking. Just straight off. *I am sorry and ashamed.*"

"Don't say ashamed."

"Why not? I am."

"Of course you are, but just hold back on *ashamed* until you *have* to use it and then — use it."

"What do you think is going to happen?"

"I think nothing," Teddy said. "Not just because everyone's so relieved that Ruby is found — but really, Jess, the only mistake you made was shutting the door to the bathroom."

"Well, pretty big mistake. And I tried on all that stuff of Whee's."

"That was a small mistake, not criminal, not dangerous. Sort of like shoplifting, but from your sister."

The spirit in room 618 was jubilant.

"I'm really sorry, Danny," Jess said.

"Me too, Jess. Really sorry I put you in that position."

And that was that.

Aldie ordered room service for breakfast with extra coffee, since it was already seven thirty and no one had slept. Whee went for a run with Victor along the water, and Delilah went to get her hair done in an upsweep.

Jess and Teddy turned over on the bed and slept as close together as they could get without suffocating.

"I'll hear about it later," Jess said when they woke up. It was still morning, a bright and perfect day.

"Maybe you won't, Jess," Teddy said. "Maybe everyone will talk about losing and finding Baby Ruby but they won't blame you. Not like you think they will."

"The only thing that really upsets me is that everyone else is holding Baby Ruby — did you notice? " Jess said. "Even you, Teddy, who doesn't even want to hold her."

"Don't take it personally, Jess."

"Are you kidding? Of course it's personal, Teddy. They don't want me near her."

Teddy leaned back against a pillow, stretched, took a cigarette from the side table.

"Is this a smoking room?" she asked.

"Nonsmoking," Jess said.

"Maybe you're right," Teddy said, putting the cigarette back in the package. "Maybe they are punishing you the way they can. But who knows? Sometimes things change pretty fast."

Delilah wandered around the bedroom doing this and that, zipping up Beet's dress, using a safety pin to replace the broken clasp on Teddy's short lavender sundress.

Delilah was wearing a matching pink-flowered bikini and bra.

"Hope you have another outfit to wear for the wedding, Mom," Teddy said.

"What do you mean?"

"Not the best look for your figure right now."

"I bought two dresses — one is a little wider in the bottom than the dress I had on last night and the other is formfitting — both are rose-colored, so you girls can choose."

"I can choose already," Teddy said. "Wider in the bottom."

Jess got her dress out of the closet and held it up to look at it one more time, checking the shape without her in it. Her dress was lavender as well, not the same dress as Teddy's since her sister's was made for someone so skinny she could be mistaken for a pencil, but straight around Jess's belly so the rolls of flesh were hidden. It had a square neck and a floaty hemline, and she had strappy shoes in lavender with high heels.

Whatever was going on with her body, Jess could always count on looking good in heels.

"Don't think that, Jess," Teddy said.

"Think what?" Jess asked.

"About your baby fat," she said. "I can tell what you're thinking."

"Your baby fat is disappearing," Delilah said. "Check it out."

"I did," Jess said. "In the shower. There's been no change since yesterday."

But since yesterday, there had been other changes for Jess. At least one, she thought, sitting on the end of the bed in her towel.

"If Danny asked me now to babysit Ruby, I'd say no. Even if he whined and cried and Delilah told me how he had to deliver the important speech at the rehearsal dinner, I'd say *No*."

"It wasn't Danny's fault," Delilah said. "He was giving the important speech at the rehearsal dinner."

"A doozy," Teddy said. "I was on the edge of my seat."

"I didn't say it was Danny's fault, Mom. It was mine," Jess said. "I'm practicing NO. No, no, no, no, no, no, no, no. No, thank you. No, I'm sorry. No, but thanks for asking. That's what I'm practicing to be — a little more like Teddy and a little less like me."

"And since we're on the subject of me, Mom, I am done with the Home for Girls with Problems, just for your information," Teddy said, putting on wild-grape blush.

"Not your choice," Delilah said.

"My choice, Mom."

"We'll see," she said.

"I'm not going back," Teddy said, sitting down with Jess in the over-sized chair in front of the television, which was off.

"I know," Jess said. "Everything is kind of different now, isn't it?"

"We're like heroes."

"Well, you are, Teddy," Jess said. "Not me."

"Wrong, Jess. You are amazing."

Whee came out of the bathroom in her dress, her hair up, her cheeks flushed, her eyes bright blue as the afternoon.

"Wooo wooo," Teddy said.

"Gorgeous," Delilah said. "My baby girl. You are breathtaking."

"Not bad, Whee," Danny said. "Good enough to get married this afternoon."

On the bed, Beet was holding Baby Ruby, who was softly sleeping in her arms.

"Does Dad get to see you before you walk down the aisle?" Danny asked.

"Nope. Not Dad and not Victor. Just you," Whee said. "And, Mom, put on your dress. You're going to a wedding."

"So now we go downstairs, right?" Danny asked.

"Downstairs and across the lobby, where there's a room right next to the garden where we'll stay until the music starts to play."

"And then what?"

"Then we walk in to the music, Danny, except you stand outside and pass out programs. First Mom, then Beet, and then my three girls. I come in last with Aldie, who will be crying although I've asked him not to."

"Who are your girls?" Delilah asked, surprised. "Did you change your mind? I thought it was Teddy and Jess."

"And Baby Ruby," Whee said. "I added one."

"Ruby? A bridesmaid?" Delilah said. "I thought Beet was holding her and sitting next to me."

"No, Beet isn't holding her. She's walking down the aisle with Teddy and Jess."

Beet had gotten up and was walking across the room with Baby Ruby.

Jess was standing with Teddy next to the door.

"Here, Jess," Beet said, putting Baby Ruby in Jess's arms. "Whee thought that you should carry the littlest bridesmaid down the aisle."

And she put Ruby, Baby Ruby, in Jess's arms.

ACKNOWLEDGMENTS

Huge thanks to Nick Thomas — for his ear for voice in fiction, his great editorial skills, and his generosity of spirit.

To Carrie Hannigan, my former and longtime children's book agent and friend, whose sensitivity and care with a writer is remarkable . . . years of thanks for many things.

To Lilly Palmer for being the first child reader of this book.

And always to my own grandchildren from two to eleven — Theo and Noah and Izy, Henry and Julian, Padget and Eliza, Aden and Elodie, who all eat up books like cupcakes.

ABOUT THE AUTHOR

Susan Richards Shreve has published a memoir, fourteen novels, and thirty books for children, including *Blister* and *The Lovely Shoes*. She is a professor at George Mason University and has received several grants for fiction, including grants from the Guggenheim Foundation and the National Endowment for the Arts. Susan lives in Washington, DC.

THIS BOOK WAS EDITED BY ARTHUR LEVINE AND DESIGNED BY ELLEN DUDA. THE TEXT WAS SET IN VENDETTA, A TYPEFACE DESIGNED BY JOHN DOWNER, AND THE DISPLAY TYPE WAS SET IN INCISED 901, A TYPEFACE DESIGNED BY ROGER EXCOFFON. THE BOOK WAS PRINTED AND BOUND AT RR DONNELLEY IN CRAWFORDSVILLE, INDIANA. PRODUCTION WAS SUPERVISED BY ELIZABETH KRYCH, AND MANUFACTURING WAS SUPERVISED BY SHANNON RICE.